GULLTIDE

A LitRPG Nature-Sim by Adam C Mitchell

Book 1 Of the Lives Of The Animara

Copyright Notice

First Published in Shropshire - United Kingdom 2024
Copyright © by Adam C. Mitchell
All rights reserved. No part of this publication may be reproduced, stored, or introduced into a retrieval system, or transmitted in any form, or by any means (electronic, mechanical, photocopying, audio/visual or otherwise) without prior written permission from the Primary Author - unless a brief quote from said work is used as part of a review.

Both the rights of Adam C Mitchell and the herein designated authors of this work have been asserted by them by the Copyrights © Designs and Patents Act/ The Intellectual Property Act 1988-2023.

This book is sold subject to the condition that it shall not, by any way of trade or otherwise, be lent, re-sold, hired out, or otherwise circulated without the author's prior consent. This book may not be put in any form of alternate binding or cover without the above author's clause being met. All clauses mentioned also apply to the subsequent purchaser of the book.

Acknowledgement

I want to express my heartfelt gratitude to everyone who patiently listened to my musings and distractions throughout this journey. Your steadfast support and understanding have made this book possible. A special thank you to my family for standing by me as this fictitious world unfolded. Your patience has allowed many more stories to take shape. Thank you for your kindness!

Appendix

What is an Amimara?

Animara (Animaridae) are a diverse and highly adaptive clade of creatures found across various habitats in the Animara world. Characterised by their unique ability to harness elemental powers, Animara exhibits multiple physiological and behavioural adaptations, including flight, aquatic locomotion, and manipulating natural elements such as fire, water, and electricity. Many, but not all, Animara undergo a variety of processes that can trigger an evolution stage, wherein they transform into more advanced forms with enhanced capabilities.

These creatures demonstrate significant intelligence and exhibit complex behaviours essential for survival in the wild. Animara taxonomy is classified as multiple types based on their elemental abilities, such as Fire, Water, Grass, Electric, and Earth; these are the core types but as with most things, there are subsets of these. Each type encompasses species with similar traits and ecological niches, contributing to the rich biodiversity and intricate ecosystems of the Animara world.

Chapter One: A Coastal Breeze

In the early light of autumn's last dawn, nestled within the tranquil confines of the nature reserve, a Gulltide stirs in its carefully constructed nest. As the first rays of sunlight pierce the canopy, its pale yellow eyes flicker open, reflecting the soft hues of the awakening sky. With a graceful stretch of its blue-grey wings, adorned with distinctive dark wingtips, it prepares for the day's endeavours. The Gulltide's keen eyes scan the surroundings, a testament to its exceptional vision, ever ready to spot the first signs of sustenance.

The coastal breeze rustles through the vegetation lining its nest, a humble yet secure structure crafted with meticulous precision from twigs, leaves, and other natural debris. This adaptable avian marvel, thriving in diverse environments, from rugged cliffs to serene wetlands, epitomises resilience and adaptability. As the morning chorus of the reserve begins, the Gulltide rises, its powerful wings poised to embrace the coastal glide. Each stroke propels it forward with remarkable efficiency, a seamless blend of elegance and survival in nature's grand tapestry.

The Gulltide is a master of the skies, traversing great distances with ease. Today, like every day, it will embark on a relentless search for food, slowly building itself for what is to come. As autumn paints the landscape with hues of amber and gold, the coastal pickings grow slim, yet the Gulltide remains undeterred in its quest for companionship.

Its primary bond, the monogamous mate, like many Animara of the sea, has travelled to distant waters to prepare for the coming mating season. The mate's absence means the Gulltide must embark on a determined search, navigating the shoreline with unwavering resolve to find and reunite with its counterpart.

As the mating season approaches, the Gulltide's journey becomes one of reconnecting with its familiar partner and returning to the nest to prepare for the new cycle of life. Each sweep of its keen eyes, each graceful glide above the waves, speaks of a relentless pursuit of nourishment. The autumn winds, carrying a hint of winter's chill, rustle through its feathers, a reminder of the harsh season ahead.

Yet, in this magnificent dance of survival, the Gulltide exemplifies nature's resilience, adapting to the ebb and flow of life with a quiet tenacity. Even as the bounty of autumn fades, it remains a master of the skies, ever vigilant, ever striving, a testament to the enduring spirit of the wild.

As it meticulously searches the shorelines and peers into numerous rock pools, the Gulltide finally spots its first meal of the day. A small gastropod, nestled comfortably in its watery haven, remains blissfully unaware of the imminent danger. With swift precision, the Gulltide strikes, demonstrating the relentless and unyielding cycle of nature, where predator and prey coexist in a delicate balance.

This fleeting moment, though seemingly insignificant, epitomises the intricate and awe-inspiring dance of life on the rugged coastal landscape. As the Gulltide delicately fishes the gastropod out of its rock-pool sanctuary with its finely tuned beak, it hovers momentarily above the rugged shoreline. In a calculated move, it ascends and then releases its shelled prey onto the rocks below, shattering the protective casing with a sharp crack.

As the shell shatters, the Gulltide swiftly descends, landing with grace and precision. In a matter of moments, it eagerly devours the exposed morsel, savouring the modest yet vital 75 calories. This brief but successful hunt underscores the Gulltide's remarkable ingenuity and adaptability. Each meal, however small, is a crucial step in its daily struggle for survival, showcasing the resilience and intelligence of this avian marvel in the ever-changing coastal landscape of the reserve.

The Gulltide continues its search, exploring several more rock pools along the rugged shoreline. With practised skill, it discovers additional gastropods and smaller aquatic creatures that inhabit these miniature ecosystems. Using the same ingenious method, it deftly breaks through shells and spines to access the tender meat within.

Research has shown that Gulltides often cover several miles within a few hours, and this morning's foraging, spanning around ten miles of shoreline, yields an additional 150 calories, a modest yet essential boost to its energy reserves. As dawn gives way to the day, the Gulltide gracefully lands on a dry rock, taking a well-deserved rest from its morning hunt, embodying the quiet perseverance of nature's cycle.

Following its morning hunt, the Gulltide alights upon a sunlit rock, ready for a crucial period of restoration. The coastal winds have stirred up sand and dust that settles on its plumage. With methodical precision, the Gulltide uses its beak to meticulously realign and smooth each feather.

This intricate process of preening is not merely for appearance, but vital for maintaining the waterproof integrity and aerodynamic efficiency of its plumage. As it preens, the Gulltide showcases a masterful blend of resilience and grace, preparing itself for the demands of its ceaseless journey along the rugged shoreline.

As you observe this particular Gulltide, you may notice a small but significant device affixed to its leg—a sophisticated Animara Data Tag. This cutting-edge technology is designed by the Animara Conservation Commission to track its, for want of a better term, "reunion pilgrimage," capturing every mile flown and calorie consumed until it reaches its familial breeding grounds.

Fascinatingly, the data collected is organised in a manner reminiscent of how captured and tamed Animara are monitored in the world of Animara Taming and the battle leagues. Translating the Gulltide's natural behaviours into known Animara move types, etc.

Additionally, the tag features a rudimentary XP gauge and Level system, providing insight into the bird's progress. This blend of natural observation and technological innovation offers a unique perspective on the Gulltide's remarkable journey.

For our initial look, we shall see the Gulltide's stats through this system from the day before the tag was activated, incorporating this morning's first activities of the day, resulting in the base stats for the rest of the journey. As the Gulltide continues to preen and dry itself from its morning's efforts, we will seize this moment to examine the initial stats of this extraordinary flying Animara, uncovering the details of its epic journey.

Animara Metrics Table			
Name: Gulltide Scientific Name: Larus Aquatilis Type: Water/Flying Height: 55cm (21.65 inches) Weight: 1,750 grams (3.86 pounds) Wingspan: 1.5 metres (4.92 feet)			
	Yesterday	Today	Total
Current HP Score	51.67%	64.17%	64.17%
Total Flight Time	4 Hours	4 Hours	8 Hours
Distance Travelled	20 Miles	10 Miles	30 Miles
Calories Consumed	200 Cal	150 Cal	350 Cal
Current XP Score	893.5 XP	746.8 XP	1640.3 XP
XP Needed For next level	N/A	N/A	1359.7 XP

Consider an average Gulltide embarking on its daily routine. Each day, its flight time, distance travelled, and calorie intake are precisely recorded. For instance, the Gulltide may fly for the full four-hour goal, cover thirty miles, and consume 350 calories—slightly surpassing the daily intake target. These metrics are compared against ideal benchmarks set by the system. The stat system assigns experience points, or XP, based on how well a Gulltide, in the case of our series, 'our tagged Gulltide' performs relative to these goals. Flying time and distance are evaluated against set targets, while the calories consumed contribute to health restoration. In this example, the Gulltide's extra calorie intake helps to boost its health, allowing it to earn maximum XP for the day's efforts.

Health is a critical factor, as a higher health percentage means more XP is earned. The ultimate aim for the Gulltide is to reach Level 10, a prestigious milestone believed to be optimal for mating and the breeding season. By consistently meeting or exceeding daily benchmarks, the Gulltide progresses toward this revered level, ensuring its readiness for future generations.

The stat system, therefore, plays a pivotal role in translating these measurements into understandable scales and levels, guiding each Gulltide's journey through its developmental stages.

Though typically a solitary traveller, our Gulltide occasionally immerses itself in the vibrant social tapestry of its kind. Amidst the rugged cliffs and sweeping shores, it engages in spirited interactions with fellow Gulltides—calling out with resonant cries, performing intricate displays of plumage, and forging fleeting bonds. Yet, in the grand scheme of its life, only the bonds with its young and mate hold significance. Even if its mate is miles away, their connection remains steadfast and unyielding.

As the crisp autumn morning unfolds along the rugged coastline, the Gulltide leaves behind the lively gatherings on the shoreline and soars back over a distance of one and a half miles to its nest, tucked away among the towering cliff faces. These cliffs, majestic and imposing, rise above with their dark rock veins and streaks of white, creating a dramatic mosaic of ledges and crevices. Here, in the tranquil sanctuary of its high perch, the Gulltide finds respite from the brisk wind and the muted hues of autumn, which envelop the landscape in a serene embrace.

The coastline itself is a striking blend of sandy stretches interspersed with driftwood and pebbled areas, where land and sea meet in a dramatic dance. This secluded alcove, sheltered and serene, offers an ideal nesting site for our avian friend. As the sun arcs towards the afternoon, the Gulltide's instincts will stir it from its rest, compelling it to heed the ancient call to seek out its familial counterpart and set forth once more on its journey, ready to embrace the adventures that lie ahead.

Chapter Two: The Relentless Chase

As the final autumn afternoon bathes the landscape in golden hues, our tagged Gulltide stirs from its rest. The air is crisp, infused with the briny scent of the sea. With a graceful stretch of its wings, the gull takes flight, cruising over the ocean's expanse near the cliffs.

Retracing its morning route with practised precision, the clever avian scans the waters below. Fortune favours its keen eyes, and soon it spots two succulent gastropods nestled in the tide. With a swift, calculated dive, the Gulltide seizes its reward and descends to the ground to feast.

But tranquillity and the promise of a swift meal are fleeting. The sudden, piercing call of a Falcomber shatters the serene calm, sending tremors of alarm through the gull. The sight of the menacing predator triggers an instinctive response.

The gull ascends into the sky with a manoeuvre akin to 'Air Cutter,' desperately clutching its food.

The Falcomber launches a relentless barrage of 'Wing Attacks,' each swoop executed with deadly precision.

The Gulltide, manoeuvring with extraordinary agility, counters with its own 'Air Cutter,' skillfully deflecting the Falcomber's burning strikes.

As the dramatic chase unfolds, the Gulltide retaliates with a series of swift 'Peck' attacks, attempting to ward off its relentless foe. Yet, the Falcomber proves tenacious, landing a decisive burning blow that reduces the Gulltide's health to 25%.

With a final, determined surge, the Gulltide climbs rapidly to safety, reaching ninety feet in under a minute. Amid the chaos, the precious morsel slips from its grasp, plummeting into the sea, claimed once more by the depths. Triumphantly, the Gulltide emerges victorious, having evaded and outmanoeuvred its relentless predator.

This gripping encounter underscores the extraordinary survival instincts of these avian Animara, vividly illustrating the delicate and dynamic balance of predator and prey in their aerial world.

As our tagged Gulltide regains its composure, it harnesses the autumnal wind currents to maintain its altitude. Gliding effortlessly, with the aid of its innate 'Coastal Glide,' the gull utilises the coastal breeze to enhance its flight.

Drawing on this remarkable skill, the Gulltide achieves a glide speed of thirty-five miles per hour, surpassing its normal flight speed of around twenty-eight miles per hour. Each graceful loop spans 100 metres as the gull circles its surroundings.

With no sign of the Falcomber, it stretches its wings and, propelled by this innate ability, descends smoothly to tree level, and very soon towards some mudflats in search of food. This energy-efficient technique allows the Gulltide to cover substantial distances with minimal effort, embodying the elegance and efficiency of the coastal skies.

As our intrepid Gulltide descends onto the coastal mudflats, it is greeted by a lively tableau. A group of Ottersnout, their sleek, dark fur glistening in the fading light, frolic energetically as they dive and surface among the mudflats. Their playful antics stir up clouds of sediment, transforming the once-clear waters into a swirling, opaque maelstrom. This tumultuous activity obscures the Gulltide's view, complicating its quest for food and scattering smaller creatures, disrupting the delicate balance of life on the mudflats.

Undeterred, the Gulltide navigates this dynamic and chaotic landscape with a keen eye and resolute spirit. From the height of the afternoon until the onset of dusk, it diligently forages, covering up to 500 metres along the mudflats as it sifts through the murky waters and sediment.

As the sun begins to set, painting the sky with hues of amber and gold, the Gulltide's perseverance pays off. It manages to secure a modest but nourishing feast—five worms, grubs, and large coastal insects, accompanied by four clams.

This assortment provides the Gulltide with an essential bounty of approximately 250 to 350 calories, replenishing its energy reserves and preparing it for the coming night. As the amber hues of the setting sun gradually fade, the Gulltide finds a moment of serene solitude.

With the horizon dissolving into twilight, the gull tucks its head beneath its wing, enveloped in the warmth and security of its plumage. Here, on this quiet, elevated refuge, the Gulltide rests undisturbed, poised for a peaceful night, while the coastal realm transitions from the vibrant hues of day to the soothing calm of evening, awaiting the promise of a new dawn.

As the first day of winter breaks over the coastal mudflats, our Gulltide awakens to a world transformed. The early morning air is crisp and frosty, with a biting chill that heralds the onset of the season.

A delicate veil of frost adorns the mudflats, shimmering faintly in the pale light of dawn. The once-soft mud has hardened, and the shallow pools are rimmed with ice, creating a stark and challenging environment for foraging. The cold temperatures force the Gulltide to expend more energy to maintain its body heat, leading to quicker fatigue and reduced flight efficiency.

As the bird stretches its wings and surveys the frosted landscape, it faces the dual challenge of navigating the icy terrain while conserving energy for the demanding foraging ahead. The icy conditions will make food scarcer and the morning's search more arduous, as the Gulltide adapts to the new challenges winter brings to its habitat.

As the chill of winter settles over the coastal mudflats, our Gulltide spreads its wings and glides gracefully to investigate an unexpected opportunity. A Boartusk, driven by the scarcity of food, has ventured into the Gulltide's domain.

Though not a typical resident of such habitats, the boar's powerful snout deftly roots through the mud, unearthing a trove of roots, tubers, and hidden invertebrates. Remarkably, the boar appears to dig up sections rich in foodstuffs deliberately, seemingly unaware of the gull's presence.

The Gulltide, ever the opportunist, descends to feast on the exposed bounty. Thanks to the boar's industrious foraging, the gull manages to consume around 400 calories, a vital morning feast that will bolster its reserves of fat and muscle, essential for enduring the colder months and maintaining its agile flight in this challenging season.

This intriguing symbiotic relationship exemplifies the extraordinary and sometimes enigmatic bonds within the Animara. The cooperation between the Boartusk and the Gulltide is a vivid testament to nature's intricate web of mutual benefit and interdependence. It's a dynamic interaction that underscores how species can adapt and assist one another, a phenomenon that never ceases to fascinate and inspire.

Sadly, this harmonious relationship stands in stark contrast to our struggles as humans to grasp and apply similar principles of cooperation and mutual aid. In our quest for progress, we often overlook the wisdom embedded in such natural alliances. As we face growing environmental challenges, there is much to learn from the seamless, cooperative strategies observed in the natural world. The lessons of the Animara remind us of the potential for more sustainable and harmonious ways of living, highlighting a path that humanity has yet to fully embrace.

For the coming week, our resilient Gulltide will steadfastly remain within a 500-metre perimeter of its sandy dune refuge, meticulously navigating the cold, wintery landscape in search of sustenance. This area, once a vibrant feeding ground, now demands careful exploration as the gull diligently forages to build up its fat reserves. Each day, it will methodically sift through the frosted mudflats and scrutinise the disturbed patches left by the Boartusk, seeking out every morsel.

This crucial period of concentrated feeding allowed the Gulltide to accumulate just short of 1,000 calories, vital for fortifying itself before the next demanding leg of its journey. As the days progressed, the Gulltide's persistent efforts ensured it was well-prepared to tackle the challenges ahead, poised to take flight with renewed vigour and strength, ready to embrace the next phase of its epic journey.

Chapter Three: Guardians of the Wild

As the relentless winter winds ravage the landscape, our Gulltide is driven to venture deeper into the shadowy expanse of the nature reserve's woodlands. The icy gusts whip around it, demanding every ounce of its strength to stay aloft. Amidst this harsh, unyielding environment, a desperate call pierces the wind—an urgent, heart-wrenching cry from a fellow gull.

Instinctively drawn to the source, the Gulltide descends through the dense canopy of trees to the forest floor below. There, amid the frost-kissed undergrowth, it finds a grievously injured elder, its feathers stained with blood and its form trembling weakly.

The sight of its kin in such peril ignites a powerful protective drive within the Gulltide. Typically a solitary and independent creature, it now assumes a defensive posture, every feather bristling in readiness. The palpable threat that has caused such suffering is evident, and our Gulltide stands steadfast, prepared to face any danger that might emerge from the surrounding gloom.

In this poignant moment of solidarity, it transcends its solitary nature, becoming a vigilant guardian. This transformation embodies the profound strength and unity essential for survival in the harsh and unforgiving winter wilderness.

In the majestic interplay of nature and companionship, the profound bond between Animara trainers and their Gulltides reveals an extraordinary tale of unity and strength. This deep connection, forged through countless moments of shared experience and mutual respect, transforms the Gulltide into a remarkable ally—one that commands reverence and admiration from any Animara trainer.

Each training session, and each challenge faced together, deepen this bond, enhancing the Gulltide's loyalty and infusing it with fierce dedication. As trainers invest their time and care, nurturing this relationship with patience and understanding, the Gulltide responds with unwavering resilience and extraordinary courage. It soars with renewed vigour, embodying the spirit of its trainer's devotion.

This remarkable synergy between humans and Animara transcends mere partnership; it is a testament to the power of shared aspirations and trust. In the harmonious unity of their efforts, both trainer and Gulltide rise to new heights, revealing the true potential of their alliance. The Gulltide, once a solitary force of nature, becomes an indispensable companion, its strength magnified through the profound bond it shares with its trainer in the ever-enchanting world of Animara.

As a winter chill envelops the forest, casting an ethereal mist upon the landscape, the Gulltide stands as a vigilant guardian to its elder gull. From the dense, shadowy vegetation, a formidable presence emerges—the Shadefang, a master of stealth and deadly precision. This serpent, with its scales gleaming like polished jewels, embodies a grave danger to the airborne Animara.

The Shadefang, an inhabitant of the lofty treetops, wields its extraordinary adaptation with chilling efficiency. Its venomous spray, a marvel of evolutionary design, enables it to incapacitate any bird that ventures too close to its high perch.

With the serene beauty of the forest juxtaposed against the relentless predatory prowess of the Shadefang, Gulltide faces a dire challenge. It must fight for its very life, for when a Shadefang sights a potential meal, its pursuit is unyielding.

In the dense forest clearing, the scene is set for a dramatic confrontation. Our tagged Gulltide hovers just inches above the ground, its sharp eyes fixed anxiously on the wounded elder it guards. Below, the menacing Shadefang, its scales glinting with a sinister sheen, slithers closer, drawn to the vulnerable prey.

Our Gulltide makes a swift, determined dive, its beak pecking aggressively, forcing the serpent to recoil in surprise. The Shadefang, however, hisses and retaliates with a sudden lunge, its fangs sinking into the Gulltide's wing.

The sharp pain causes the Gulltide to falter momentarily, but with a fierce cry, it regains its resolve. Hovering with remarkable agility, our little Gulltide unleashes a flurry of rapid strikes, its beak darting with precision. The relentless assault drives the Shadefang back, its slithering retreat growing more frantic.

Despite its injuries, our Gulltide remains steadfast, its wings beating with a mix of exhaustion and determination. With a final wary glance, the Shadefang retreats into the shadows, leaving the Gulltide and its elder.

A glance at the Gulltide's data tag reveals that the Shadefang's venom has inflicted significant damage. This common poison, frequently noted by the Animara Healthcare Federation, will diminish our Gulltide's health and experience by 15% each hour until treated.

While the bite will heal in time, the poison's effects are far more dire and require immediate attention. As the next hour passes, the urgency for medical aid grows. In the wild, however, only the Animara's instincts will offer the much-needed reprieve it seeks. While foraging for food is crucial, the quest for medicinal aid now takes precedence.

Research and observations have shown that Larus Aquatilis *(of the Gulltide family)* has exhibited remarkable behaviour. It has been observed consuming seeds from certain plants, which the Gulltide uses to address a range of issues—from digestive troubles to more pressing needs, such as the anti-venom properties found in Thistleberries *(Cirsium Nigra)*. This instinctual search for medicinal aid highlights the adaptability and resourcefulness of birds in managing their health, ensuring that even in the wild, they find ways to heal and survive.

As the poison saps our Gulltide's vitality as another hour passes, the urgency of the situation becomes starkly apparent. According to the data tag, the next forty minutes unfold as a crucial quest for survival. Roles reversed and accompanied by its elder, our tagged Gulltide, with unwavering determination, embark on a foraging journey through the forest that spans twelve miles both in the air and on the ground among the shrubs and vegetation.

It eventually seeks out the rare and precious seeds known for their healing properties. Among them, Cirsium nigra stands out, celebrated for its antioxidant and blood-purifying qualities, offering vital immune support against the toxic effects of poison. After an exhaustive search and careful preparation, our Gulltide consumes these life-saving seeds. Shortly thereafter, the elder Gulltide, invigorated and renewed, takes flight to continue its journey, leaving its patient to rest.

Meanwhile, our resilient Gulltide finds a peaceful refuge on a nearby hillside, resting with a hopeful heart. Trusting that nature's remedies will restore its strength and well-being in time.

After a day of rest, which also provided an opportunity to feast on nourishing fruits and insects, our Gulltide is back in the sky, invigorated and ready to resume its journey. The fruits have replenished its energy reserves by around 30 Cal, which had been depleted by its recent tangle with the Shadefang.

With renewed vigour, it follows the winding stream, guiding it out of the dense woodland. From above, the landscape unfolds, leading the Gulltide towards the expansive coastal shoreline. This brief respite has propelled our little sea-flying Animara closer to its breeding goal by gaining it another level.

As it soars towards the sunlit horizon, eager to continue its quest, the shoreline and ocean greet it with fresh winds. As it glides over the ocean, we will take a quick moment to look at its stats up to the serpentine encounter.

Animara Metrics	
Name: Gulltide Scientific Name: Larus Aquatilis Height: 55cm (21.65 inches) Weight: 1,750 grams (3.86 pounds) Wingspan: 1.5 metres (4.92 feet)	
Current HP Score	64.17%
Flight Time	4 Hours
Distance Travelled	10 Miles
Calories Consumed	150 Cal
Current XP Score	746.8XP
XP Needed For Next Level (LV3)	1359.7XP
System Notes	None at Present

Chapter Four: Wings Against the Storm

As our tagged Gulltide embarks on its aerial pilgrimage along the rugged coastline, the unforgiving winter takes its toll. A relentless coastal storm, brewing with heavy rain and fierce gales, has swept across the reserve, transforming the skies into a treacherous battleground.

For our feathered Animara, the once effortless glide over miles of open water has become an arduous struggle, each wingbeat being met with resistance. Forced to adapt, the Gulltide no longer ventures far in search of food, reducing its foraging range to mere yards. Here, in the grip of nature's fury, survival is not just a matter of instinct but a test of endurance.

We catch up with our enduring Gulltide as he scours the coastal scrublands and marshes, desperately seeking any sign of sustenance. But the relentless onslaught of winter rain has taken a heavy toll. Each gust of wind, each icy downpour, chips away at his strength. His stats have plummeted by 25%, a stark reflection of the harsh realities of survival in this unforgiving environment.

Though the Gulltide is a Water/Flying Animara, its predominant Flying type isn't built for prolonged wet conditions. It thrives in short bursts when foraging in coastal waters, but these endless downpours push its endurance to the brink. Prolonged exposure to the cold and damp, with little opportunity for proper nesting or shelter, has further eroded its vitality, dragging its stats down to a perilous 50%.

As the relentless day wanes and winter's icy grasp tightens, our Gulltide, ever resilient, braces itself against the unyielding tempest. Nature, in all its raw fury, tests the endurance of this hardy Animara. Yet it navigates the storm with an innate grace born of survival. Gale-force winds whip across the coastal cliffs, driving rain in relentless sheets as if the very elements conspire to thwart the bird's usual flight path along the rugged shoreline of the reserve.

Yet, the Gulltide, with its innate adaptability, adjusts its course with remarkable precision. Abandoning its original trajectory, it veers inland, seeking refuge in the expansive forest of the nature reserve. Here, beneath the partial protection of towering oaks and pines, the Gulltide finds a temporary haven.

The forest, cloaked in winter's muted tones, offers a stark contrast to the storm-lashed coast. The trees, though bare, provide a vital windbreak, allowing the Gulltide to navigate with greater ease. As the wind howls above, the Gulltide gracefully adjusts its flight, proving once more the incredible resilience of nature's avian travellers.

Under the leafy canopy of the ancient forest, our Gulltide, drenched and weary from the storm's relentless assault, seeks refuge among the sturdy branches of a venerable oak. Here, nestled within the protective embrace of the great tree, it begins the meticulous task of preening, carefully drying its feathers with the precision only a seasoned survivor can muster. Each movement is deliberate, an instinctual ritual vital for maintaining the waterproofing that allows it to withstand the elements.

But the forest is never still. The quiet rustle of leaves is suddenly interrupted by the unmistakable sound of a Boartusk sounder—a formidable group of *Forestis aper*—foraging with determined vigour. These wild swine are vital architects of this woodland domain, turning over the rich soil in search of truffles and mushrooms.

As they dig, they transform the forest floor, creating a dynamic environment that benefits a myriad of Animara species. Insects and seeds flourish in the disturbed earth, maintaining the delicate balance of this complex ecosystem. The Boartusks' presence, though imposing, is a reminder of the intricate web of life that thrives beneath the forest's leafy crown, where even the smallest actions ripple through the natural world.

As the sounder of Boartusk gorges itself on the feast unearthed from the forest floor, the scene quickly transforms into a vibrant gathering of life. Other Animara, both of the forest and sky, begin to filter down, drawn by the rich bounty exposed by the Boartusks' tireless foraging.

Worms, ticks, fruit, mushrooms, and truffles — each offers sustenance to a diverse array of creatures. The gentle and symbiotic nature of these Grass and Air-based Animara ensures that their gathering does not disturb or annoy the larger forest swine. Quite the opposite. The Boartusks benefit from the presence of their feathered companions, who pick at the ticks and insects Animara that might otherwise burrow into their soft underbellies and hindquarters.

It is a perfect example of nature's intricate design, where each species plays a role in the survival of others, creating a harmonious balance within this ancient woodland. Here, beneath the towering trees, the interconnectedness of life is on full display, a testament to the subtle yet powerful bonds that sustain the natural world.

Our tagged Gulltide, ever resourceful, soon joins the bustling throng of Animara gathered around the foraging Boartusks. As the sounder methodically churns through the forest floor, the Gulltide takes full advantage of the bounty left in their wake, feasting on the calorie-rich mushrooms and truffle fragments scattered amid the turned earth. For the next hour, amidst the steady rainfall from the ongoing storm, the Gulltide dines alongside its fellow forest dwellers, undeterred by the relentless weather.

Each morsel is a lifeline, vital for survival in these harsh conditions. The stat tag on our Gulltide tells the story of a successful foraging effort: around 25 grams of truffle fragments, yielding 80 valuable calories, and 220 grams of wild mushroom leftovers, providing an additional 250 calories. These 330 calories are crucial for the Gulltide, offering the energy it needs to maintain its body heat and strength, ready to face the harsh winter night ahead.

As the forest diners scatter under the relentless assault of worsening winter rains, our intrepid Gulltide once again takes to the air. The forest, shrouded in a thick curtain of rain, is an ever-changing mosaic of greens and greys, with the canopy swaying in the fierce winds. In a display of remarkable agility, the Gulltide weaves deftly through the labyrinth of trees, seeking to avoid the brunt of the storm where possible.

The relentless weather, however, does little to slow its determined flight. Covering a distance of approximately seventeen and a half miles at a steady pace of around fifteen miles per hour, the Gulltide remains steadfast in its journey. Eventually, it approaches one of the few man-made structures within the nature reserve — a Ranger Station and centre.

Perched on the edge of the forest, this humble wooden station stands resilient against the storm's wrath. As the Gulltide alights upon its roof, it discovers a haven from the tempest's fury. The sturdy wooden construct provides a much-needed sanctuary, offering protection from the relentless battering of wind and rain.

Here, sheltered from the worst of the storm, the Gulltide begins to settle into its refuge. With a practised flick, it fluffs its feathers, trapping a delicate layer of insulating air against its body to conserve warmth. As the rain drums steadily and the wind roars in a symphony of winter's might, the Gulltide finds solace in the relative calm beneath the station's roof. Here, in this small respite from nature's relentless assault, the weary bird tucks its head beneath its wing and prepares for the night, grateful for this brief sanctuary amidst the unyielding elements of winter.

Chapter Five: The Scavenger's Gamble

As the winter storm subsides and the first light of dawn creeps over the nature reserve, a tranquil, albeit frosty calm settles across the landscape. The Ranger Station, now glistening with a delicate layer of frost, stands serene amidst the stillness. The forest, once battered by the storm's fury, awakens slowly, each tree and leaf coated in sparkling ice crystals.

The Gulltide, having weathered the tempest in its wooden sanctuary, emerges into a world reborn. The cold air is crisp and invigorating, promising a new day of survival and renewal as the reserve stirs to life beneath the clear, wintry sky.

As the storm's wrath diminishes and the first light of dawn gently caresses the nature reserve, a profound stillness blankets the frost-tinged landscape. The Ranger Station, now draped in a delicate, crystalline layer, stands resolute amidst the serene, wintry forest.

Emerging from its haven, the Gulltide ascends into the crisp morning air, its keen gaze surveying the frost-kissed terrain below. It embarks on a meticulous five-mile search for sustenance, its wings carving through the clear, cold sky. Yet, the harsh winter has obscured the forest's natural bounty. Ever the hopeful hunter, the Gulltide resorts to what has become an increasingly common strategy—seeking sustenance amidst the traces of human activity.

As the morning light glimmers across the frost-clad Ranger Station, the Gulltide hovers nearby, its wings beating steadily in the crisp winter air. It circles the station and its surroundings with a vigilant gaze, observing the ebb and flow of human activity below.

This solitary sentinel of the sky watches the comings and goings of its human counterparts with a blend of curiosity and patience. Finally, it descends to a nearby picnic area, where the true impact of human presence is starkly revealed. Among the remnants of human leisure, the Gulltide encounters the tangible imprint we leave upon the natural world, an intersection that proves both a blessing and a curse for the Animara.

Here, the convergence of our lives with theirs highlights a complex relationship, where human activity offers opportunities, yet also poses challenges to the delicate balance of their existence.

As the Gulltide forages through the remnants of human activity in the picnic area, it eagerly pecks at the scattered plastic wrappers and discarded packaging, hoping to find a morsel of nourishment. In its determined search, the bird inadvertently swallows fragments of plastic, mistaking them for food.

Almost immediately, it begins to choke, its airway obstructed by the foreign material. Panicked, the Gulltide flaps its wings with increasing urgency, each frantic beat a desperate attempt to dislodge the obstruction, as it flails its Health drops to 15%.

As the Gulltide flails in a desperate bid for survival, its health deteriorates by another 5%. In a moment of frantic determination, the bird manages to clear its constricted airway, but the cost is severe. The struggle has taken a significant toll, causing its experience points (XP) to plummet by a dramatic 25%.

This harrowing episode underscores the perilous impact of human refuse on wildlife, where each struggle not only threatens immediate well-being but also diminishes the Gulltide's overall chances of survival in an increasingly hazardous environment. The plight of our Gulltide, choking on discarded plastic in a once idyllic picnic area, serves as a stark illustration of a broader environmental crisis. This single episode underscores a pressing reality: the impact of human negligence on the natural world.

The plastic refuse scattered across the ground not only jeopardises the health of the Gulltide here, but also highlights a disturbing trend where the presence of human waste becomes a pervasive threat to all Animara. If we, as stewards of this planet, fail to address our environmental footprint, the delicate balance of life will suffer. The distressing struggle of this Gulltide is but a poignant reminder that our actions—however small they may seem—have far-reaching consequences. To ensure the survival and thriving of the Animara, we must act decisively to protect and preserve their habitats from the encroaching perils of human waste.

But that's a sermon for another day. Despite its close call, the Gulltides' tireless pilgrimage must go on, driven by an unyielding need for sustenance. After its near-fatal encounter, it resolutely continues its search through the remnants of human activity at the visitor centre.

Amid the discarded refuse, its vigilant eyes finally discover a half-eaten sandwich. This fortuitous find yields a vital 242 calories, replenishing its energy. With its hunger momentarily sated, the Gulltide, revitalised and determined, once again takes to the air. It resumes its journey, soaring upward and onward, ever persistent in its quest for survival.

As the Gulltide devours the salvaged morsel, its health improves by 2%, a small but significant reprieve from its earlier distress. Rejuvenated, albeit temporarily, the Gulltide gathers its strength and once again takes to the sky. With renewed determination, it resumes its journey, soaring above the landscape, continuing its relentless pilgrimage for survival in a world profoundly impacted by humanity's presence.

The sea, calm and glistening under the low winter sun, stretches out in soothing hues of slate and silver. The Gulltide settles on a smooth rock, preening its feathers and surveying the tranquil surroundings. This period of rest is vital, allowing the bird to replenish its strength and prepare for the next leg of its journey.

As the Gulltide basks in the winter sun's gentle warmth, it luxuriates in the tranquil embrace of this coastal haven. The soft rays of the sun, now low in the sky, cast a golden hue across the serene bay, offering a moment of respite from the rigours of its relentless journey. Here, amidst the soothing cadence of the winter waves and the quiet rustle of frost-kissed vegetation, the Gulltide savers this rare pause.

Yet, even as it rests and rejuvenates, the bird remains acutely aware that the challenges of his journey are far from over. The path ahead is fraught with trials, but for now, the calm of this coastal refuge provides a precious interlude, allowing the Gulltide to gather strength and prepare for the arduous journey that still awaits.

Our Gulltide finally stretches its wings after a long rest in the wintering cover, where icy winds and barren landscapes have kept it grounded for weeks. As it takes to the air, its powerful wings beat rhythmically against the crisp winter sky, and the world below fades into a blur of white and grey.

Yet, something stirs deep within—an ancient call, woven into the very fabric of its being. Among the orchestral swell of avian birdsong, a distant, familiar cry resonates—a sound not heard since spring's last breath. For the second time since winter began, our Gulltide feels that irresistible pull, an instinctive urge buried deep within its core. Without hesitation, it yields to the call, allowing instinct to guide its flight into the unknown, where the promise of something forgotten yet vital awaits.

Chapter Six: Echoes on the Wind

Our tagged Gulltide takes to the air with a grace that defies the biting cold of winter. The sharp wind and icy ocean spray do little to hinder its flight, as if impervious to the elements. Rising above the rugged cliffs, Gulltide is drawn by an ancient, irresistible pull, ascending effortlessly on the winter winds.

The coastline fades from view as it soars higher, navigating the frigid gusts with precision. Then, with a sudden pivot, it dives toward the ocean, unfazed by the freezing temperatures. The gull glides over the waves, wings cutting through the spray, undeterred by the cold, as the winds carry a distant, mysterious sound that tugs at its very core.

Carried southward by the wind currents, it presses on, skimming the reserve's edge, guided by this haunting call. As it ventures deeper into the vast, untamed sea, the pull grows stronger.

With a slow, deliberate glide, our Gulltide descends toward a small coastal sandbar nestled against a remote island chain. As it approaches, the Animara's heightened senses, honed through centuries of evolution and now greatly desired by human Animara trainers, come to life.

Among all water-flying Animara, it is the Gulltides' exceptional senses that set it apart, making it invaluable in forging a well-rounded squad for the leagues. Each Animara is uniquely attuned to the world in ways beyond human comprehension, adapting and harnessing their instincts in ways we humans can barely understand.

As the Gulltide soars above the ocean, the winter wind carries a sound that tugs at its consciousness, guiding it effortlessly. With a graceful ascent, it circles the sandbars, sharp eyes scanning the patches of sparse vegetation below. Every shift of the wind and flicker of movement is noted as it searches intently for the source of the unseen force drawing it here, to this isolated stretch of sand and sea.

Despite the powerful pull guiding our Gulltide, the journey has taken a heavy toll. In what seems like a short distance to some larger flying Animara, it has pushed itself to the brink, burning through nearly 90% of the calories stored within its small body.

As the cold night approaches, with little shelter in sight, the Gulltide faces a critical decision. To survive the frigid temperatures, it instinctively begins to convert around 15% of its remaining health, and 30% of its overall calorie stores, a desperate measure to keep itself warm in the face of the relentless cold.

Every ounce of energy is precious now, as the Gulltide battles against both the dwindling reserves and the unforgiving elements. This delicate balance of survival highlights the Animara's remarkable adaptability, as it strives to endure the harsh conditions while continuing its journey into the vast, unforgiving ocean.

With little shelter on the sandbar, our Gulltide sets its sights on the nearest island in the chain, driven by the urgent need for refuge and sustenance. Battling the frigid winds, it soars toward the island, its keen eyes scanning for a haven. Finally, it locates a suitable tree, a lofty perch close to the coast but high enough to offer protection from most predatory Animara that may roam the island at night.

Here, nestled among the branches, the Gulltide finds a temporary sanctuary. As the sun dips below the horizon, it settles into its new home for the night, sheltered from the harsh elements and potential threats, while the promise of a meal waits just beyond the trees, offering a glimmer of hope in the encroaching darkness.

As the new winter morning dawns, our tagged Gulltide awakens with a deep-seated hunger. With the sun barely touching the icy horizon, it spreads its wings and catches the early morning wind currents, gliding gracefully above the small islands and the surrounding sea in search of food.

Below the surface, a much larger Animara has stirred the waters with its massive presence, agitating the waves and disorienting a school of fish. This turbulence makes the fish vulnerable and easy pickings for the massive predator's huge appetite.

Fortuitously, this chaos also benefits our hungry Gulltide. Its keen eyes detect the disturbance, and with cautious precision, it glides closer. As it approaches the tumultuous waters, it prepares to capitalise on the opportunity, hoping to replenish its energy before the day's further trials unfold.

The mighty Frostwhalor, a titan of the winter sea, breaks the surface with a graceful surge, sending ripples through the vast expanse of ice-blue water. The sudden disturbance scatters immense schools of krill, their shimmering bodies briefly illuminated in the pale light.

High above, the Gulltide, ever attuned to the symphony of the wild, catches the resonant, primal call of its colossal counterpart. For a moment, hunger is forgotten, and the bird soars upward, wings beating with renewed purpose. It sends its call into the frosty air, a silent yet potent invitation, bridging the chasm between sky and sea. The Gulltide glides in a wide, graceful circle, its eyes scanning the horizon, patiently awaiting the response that will signal the rekindling of an ancient bond.

As the Gulltide waits, its wings beat rhythmically in a twenty-metre sweep, the creature performs a delicate ballet against the icy sky. Each pass drains its dwindling energy reserves by a further 5%, a testament to the taxing nature of its call for a companion.

The magnificent Frostwhalor below, engaged in a feeding frenzy, consumes vast swaths of krill, creating a shimmering spectacle beneath the surface. Meanwhile, the remaining krill serve as a feast for a gathering of oceanic and airborne water-type Animara, their presence adding a lively, animated touch to the scene.

As the Gulltide completes its third orbit, fatigue visibly weighs on its wings, yet it persists with unwavering determination. Just as the last of its strength ebbs away, the long-awaited reply echoes through the frigid air, a beacon of connection amidst the vast, swirling wilderness.

As our tagged Gulltide succumbs to the relentless weight of fatigue, its once-majestic wings falter, struggling to maintain altitude. With each weary beat, its strength wanes, the once-proud aerial display now a desperate fight against gravity. The call it has so diligently pursued grows louder, tantalisingly close, yet the effort proves too great.

As its wings finally surrender, the Gulltide begins a slow, spiralling descent toward the frothy expanse below. The ocean's surface, alive with a feeding frenzy, roils as the Frostwhalor's immense jaws gape wide, poised to consume the remaining krill. In this dramatic plunge, the Gulltide's journey arcs toward the jaws of nature's colossal predator, a poignant reminder of the harsh realities of survival in the wild.

As the female Gulltide descends through the sky, a dazzling streak of teal and azure feathers blurs past—its partner, the very source of the resonant call that echoes through the air. The new Gulltide, with a grace befitting its kind, synchronises its flight with that of the descending companion.

The atmosphere is filled with the calming melody of the Heal Song, a rare and precious ability unique to female Gulltides. This melodic serenade, performed in moments of need, serves to heal and reinforce the bond between life partners, ensuring their connection remains steadfast. In the wild, when a female Gulltide performs Heal Song, it absorbs half of its partner's current XP in exchange for its aid. In a league battle, however, the Gulltide absorbs half of its opponent's XP instead. As the song flows, it restores 25% of the target's maximum HP and replenishes its caloric intake. This powerful, enchanting ability allows the wounded Gulltide to recover and reunite with its partner.

The harmonious convergence of their movements and the soothing melody transform a potentially chaotic descent into a serene, shared glide towards a hopeful future. As the Gulltide pair plunges toward the oceanic feeding floor, the Heal Song's effects unfold with perfect timing. With a final, graceful flap, the tagged Gulltide tucks in its wings, preparing for the plunge. Together, they dive into the vast ocean, their synchronised descent a testament to their bond. Underwater, their wings transform into powerful oars, propelling them through the azure depths toward a rich krill feast. Their beaks deftly sift through the nutrient-rich swarm, each gulp a reward for their unity. This elegant ballet of flight and underwater foraging underscores the Gulltides' deep connection.

These remarkable birds can swim underwater for up to a minute at a time, reaching depths of around sixty metres with effortless elegance. Beneath the surface, they engage in a mesmerising dance, spiralling around each other in joyful synchronisation. As they forage for krill and calorie-rich fish, each bite replenishes them with approximately 150 Calories. After consuming a total of around 609 Calories each, they are well-fueled for their journey.

With their bellies full, the pair ascends from the sea as if soaring out of the water and back into the sky. This ascent continues their mating spiral, a ritual of reconnecting and reaffirming their bond. Energised and nourished, they head back towards the mainland of the nature reserve, ready for the next chapter of their lives together. As the sun sinks below the rugged horizon, casting a golden glow over the churning sea, the pair of Gulltides glide gracefully above the waves.

Their recent feast from the abundant waters has left them content, and they now steer toward the dramatic cliffs of the reserve's coastline. These ancient, weather-beaten precipices, carved by centuries of relentless sea and wind, offer a timeworn haven. As the chill of a winter night begins to settle in, the gulls will find refuge among the crevices and ledges of these towering cliffs, where they will nestle in for a tranquil night, sheltered from the biting cold and roaring wind.

Tomorrow, they will continue their migration towards the northern fire side of the reserve, where warmer nesting grounds await. As they soar through the tranquil skies, we turn our gaze to our Gulltide's stats. The next chapter of their journey beckons with promise and anticipation.

Animara Metrics	
Name: Gulltide Scientific Name: Larus Aquatilis Height: 55cm (21.65 inches) Weight: 1,750 grams (3.86 pounds) Wingspan: 1.5 metres (4.92 feet)	
Current HP Score	64.17%
Total Flight Time	8 Hours
Distance Travelled	55 Miles
Calories Consumed	1,300 Cal
Current XP Score	2,650 XP
XP Needed For Next Level (LV3)	350 XP
System Notes	Rejoined with a monogamous life partner - XP status in flux due to the bond level being worked towards (Level 4)
Bond Level Data >>	
As Gulltide reunites with its mate the pair work to strengthen their bond. When they hit the needed level 4 they instinctively share 15% of all experience points (XP) gained daily with each other from that point on. This unique ability is their Bond Level. It is the final push before the mating season. This bond level boosts their growth and development, increasing their chances of successful breeding and survival.	

Chapter Seven: A Dance in the Winds

As dawn's pale light stretches across the winter landscape, the reunited Animara stir from their nest, their feathers fluffed against the biting cold. The frigid air seems to penetrate even their resilient plumage, urging them to act swiftly.

They stretch their wings, each movement a testament to the effort required to counter the cold's relentless grip. With a synchronised flutter and a powerful push, they take flight into the crisp morning sky. The air is sharply cold, and as they soar together, their breaths become visible puffs, mingling with the frost-kissed air.

Each beat of their wings grows more deliberate, more urgent, as the biting temperatures heighten their need for a successful foray. The icy waters below, now partially frozen, present an added challenge. This cold, however, only strengthens their resolve. As the pair work in unison, their shared goal of survival presses them onward through the harsh winter chill.

As the gulls ascend into the crisp winter sky, their azure plumage shimmers in the fading light, a testament to nature's artistry. They momentarily hover, their vibrant feathers finely tuned to detect the subtle shifts in air currents and thermal updrafts.

However, the winds are guiding them back towards the ranger station and an unforeseen seventeen-mile detour at a reduced pace of eight miles per hour. Compounding their challenges, a formidable hailstorm begins to roll in from the coast, its icy assault pummeling their wings and bodies. The relentless storm disrupts their flight, forcing them to exert extra energy to maintain their course. Each icy impact strains their small bodies, testing their endurance. Yet, with their last refuge of the cliffs receding behind them, the gulls press on with resolute determination, navigating through the tempest toward the distant northern nesting grounds.

Their remarkable resilience shines through as they battle the hail that descends in unending sheets, compelled nonetheless to follow the waning wind currents eastward. Their course now leads them towards the reserve's man-made environment, where the visitor centre and its surrounding outbuildings loom as a distant but promising refuge.

Though around five miles away, these structures promise some relief from the storm's fury. However, the approach of this man-made haven introduces new perils, with the potential for increased human activity and lurking predators. As the gulls press on through the tempest, their survival instincts guide them carefully towards this sanctuary, balancing the storm's wrath against the emerging risks and the storm's fury.

With the rooftops of the visitor centre now tantalisingly close, the Gulltides seek respite by gliding towards a nearby power line. Here, perched high above the chaos, they keenly observe the humans below, scurrying about in a frenzy to attend to their tasks. Each gust of wind and pelting hail adds to their struggle against the winter chill. Amidst the flurry of human activity, the gulls' sharp eyes spot a promising opportunity: the garbage cans left unattended, brimming with discarded morsels. Seizing this chance for nourishment, the gulls prepare to navigate the storm-tossed air towards this unexpected bounty, their instinct for survival driving them to take advantage of every fleeting opportunity amidst the small winter tempest.

In the bustling surroundings of the nature reserve's visitor centre and its outbuildings, an unexpected scavenger thrives. As the gulls take shelter on another nearby power line, their keen eyes spot a different kind of opportunist: a Gnashrat. These resilient creatures navigate the chaos of human activity with remarkable agility, their sharp senses guiding them to the discarded remnants of human life.The rubbish bins and neglected corners of the outbuildings become their foraging grounds, where they scavenge through an array of discarded food and materials.

At this intersection of nature and human presence, the Gnashrat demonstrates its remarkable adaptability, turning the refuse of civilization into a vital source of sustenance. Amidst the storm's fury and the hustle of the visitor centre, these scavengers embody the relentless drive for survival in an ever-changing environment.

With the coast seemingly clear, the pair of Gulltides descend with agile precision, their wings slicing through the air as they approach the feast of discarded food waste surrounding the visitor centre. Amidst the refuse, they uncover a half-eaten cheeseburger, a rare bounty offering them a substantial 300 calories to share between them. As they eagerly peck at the remaining morsels, their moment of triumph is abruptly shattered.

From the shadows of the refuse, an irate Gnashrat emerges, its eyes flashing with hostility. In a sudden, violent burst, it lashes out with a fierce tailwhip, striking the female Gulltide with brutal force. Her partner springs into action, positioning himself between his injured mate and the menacing Gnashrat. With fierce resolve, he readies himself for the impending clash. The stage is set for a dramatic confrontation as the Gulltide faces off against the aggressive scavenger.

Amid the tumultuous storm battering the visitor centre, a dramatic Animara battle rages around the scattered garbage bins. Our Gulltide, its feathers drenched and ruffled by the rain, battles fiercely against the relentless Gnashrat. With precision, Gulltide employs "Aqua Jet" to dart through the air and "Wing Attack" to strike at its foe, while Gnashrat retaliates with powerful "Hyper Fang" bites and swift "Quick Attack" strikes. The scene is chaotic, with rain mingling with the debris of discarded food.

In the background, our Gulltide's wounded mate perches forlornly on the edge of a nearby bin, its eyes filled with pain yet hope, watching the fierce struggle unfold. Despite the intensity of the fight, the Gulltide's persistence begins to shift the balance.

With a decisive burst of energy, Gulltide executes a perfectly timed "Air Slash," cutting through the storm and striking the Gnashrat with a decisive blow. The impact sends the Gnashrat reeling, its resolve crumbling as it hastily retreats into the stormy night. Our Gulltide, though exhausted and battered, stands victorious beside its injured partner. A testament to its bravery and resilience amid the harsh environment of the garbage-strewn battleground.

With the Gnashrat threat now vanquished, a touching display of devotion unfolds amidst the storm-tossed refuse. Our Gulltide, weary but steadfast, retrieves the remnants of the cheeseburger from the debris and offers the precious scraps to its injured mate. As she gratefully pecks at the food, her strength begins to return. This moment of selfless care underscores the deep bond between them. Once assured of his partner's well-being, Gulltide resumes his search and soon discovers a half-eaten hotdog, providing an additional 250 calories.

After consuming the hotdog, our Gulltide hops back to his wounded mate. With the hailstorm raging around them, he wraps his wings around her, enveloping them both in warmth and protection. Together, they huddle close, their shared resilience a testament to the enduring strength of their bond.

Hours have passed, blanketing the southern coast of the reserve in a relentless assault of winter hail and biting wind. The storm, an unyielding force of nature, has finally begun to wane, leaving the landscape covered in a shimmering layer of ice. Amidst this frozen tempest, the two huddled Gulltides have sought refuge, their feathers weighed down by the icy remnants of the storm. As the storm recedes, the resilient pair shake off the frost with determined flaps, preparing to take flight once more. The male Gulltide, ever vigilant and protective, remains close to his wounded mate, offering comfort and support. With the winter air currents beginning to improve, the pair set their course north-easterly, their wings slicing through the cold, crisp air. They press onward, navigating back towards the coast, their journey a testament to their unwavering spirit.

Chapter Eight: The Feast of the Winter Sea

As the pair of avian Animara fly over forty miles, their wings gracefully carving through the slowly warming coastal air, they only pause briefly when the wind currents waver. Their journey is a testament to their mastery of the skies.

Meanwhile, the dedicated rangers on the reserve have made a subtle yet significant adjustment to their stat tags, expanding their radius with great precision. This careful modification ensures that, as the pair reaches their intricate Bond level, their statistics will merge seamlessly into a unified profile. This refined integration reflects their profound connection.

As the pair of Gulltides glide further east on the warm, embracing air currents, they arrive in the temperate sanctuary of the reserve's coastal stretch. Here, amidst the gentle climate, this monogamous pair has chosen to make their temporary home.

Their keen eyes soon detect a vital bounty: a shimmering school of Mackerlure. These sleek, torpedo-shaped fish, their scales glinting with an iridescent blue-green sheen, are a nutritional powerhouse. Each Mackerlure is packed with around 200 calories, thanks to its rich, oily nature. This high-calorie content is crucial for the Gulltides, providing the essential energy needed to strengthen their bond and sustain them through their time here.

The pair of Gulltides have chosen a tranquil sandy beach for their nesting site, skillfully adapting to their surroundings. Using a natural depression in the sand, they create a rudimentary nest, a simple yet effective strategy for protection. The gentle rise of the sand offers a modicum of shelter from the elements and predators, while the open expanse of the beach provides an unobstructed view of their surroundings. Here, amidst the rhythmic lapping of the waves and the whisper of the breeze, the male Gulltide forages for long grasses and the like to build their temporary home.

As the male Gulltide completes the construction of their temporary nest on the beach, he arranges the final pieces of driftwood and seaweed with meticulous care, shaping the depression in the sand into a snug, secure haven. Satisfied with his work, he steps back to admire the result.

The female Gulltide then begins her enchanting courtship dance, her feathers catching the sunlight as she moves. She performs a graceful ballet of wing flaps and rhythmic head-bobs, each motion a tender expression of her love, affection, and desire to build a future together. The male responds by mirroring her movements, their synchronised dance a heartfelt declaration of mutual devotion. In their tranquil beachside nest, this dance becomes a profound avian declaration of "I love you."

Embarking on a journey ten miles from the shore along the reserve's eastern coastline, we are embraced by the ocean's warmth. As dawn's first light gently graces the tranquil beach, the Gulltide pair make their appearance, their feathers aglow with the golden hues of sunrise. They venture into the inviting waters, where the winter's chill is tempered by the reserve's geothermal wonders. Remarkably, volcanic activity from the island's northern reaches has bestowed an unexpectedly spring-like warmth upon these eastern waters.

This extraordinary warmth has triggered a remarkable resurgence of marine life. Schools of Mackerlure—fish the Gulltide have been hunting since they first settled here—team in the nutrient-rich waters.

Energised by this seasonal bounty, the Gulltide dive and skim through the invigorated sea, consuming an impressive 650 calories in their diligent foraging. After their third dive, their hunger satisfied and spirits lifted, they make their way back to the shore. On the sunlit beach, they engage in the essential ritual of drying off and preening each other. This behaviour not only cleans their feathers but also strengthens their bond, preparing them for their next venture.

Over the next three days, they will repeat their ten-mile flight and feast on the bountiful Mackerlure, making this remarkable journey up to three times a day, ensuring their well-being and thriving in this vibrant coastal sanctuary.

After a final foraging expedition along their familiar route, the two Gulltides settle on the sunlit beach to bask in the warmth. With their feathers still damp from the day's dives, they find a sandy stretch and begin their sunning ritual. They spread their wings wide, allowing the sun's rays to penetrate through their plumage, which helps to dry their feathers and regulate their body temperature. Occasionally, they stretch one wing or leg, adjusting their position to capture the optimal warmth.

Unbeknownst to them, this tranquil scene is observed from the long grasses at the beach's edge. Concealed in the shadows, a patient predator watches intently, its gaze fixed on the unsuspecting pair. The Gulltide's serene sunning, a calming end to their active day, contrasts sharply with the hidden, deliberate tension that stalks them from the periphery, revealing the ever-present balance of life and survival.

Unaware of the lurking danger only a few feet away, the Gulltide pair prepare to take flight once more. Having soaked up the sun's warmth, they stretch their wings and ascend into the sky, departing from their familiar oceanic foraging route. This time, they follow the coastline, soaring gracefully on the warmed air currents that guide them northward.

As they travel approximately twenty miles along the sunlit edge of the land, their effortless flight showcases their remarkable adaptation to the environment. Meanwhile, a hidden predator remains concealed in the shadows, observing their departure with patient and silent vigilance, a stark reminder of nature, it has caught their scent and follows all the while stalking a possible meal. As the Gulltide couple glide over the warming coastline, their sharp eyes catch sight of a subtle disturbance in the water—a telltale wake trailing behind a ranger's boat.

With the grace and precision of masterful aviators, they descend from the heights, wings adjusting to the shifting currents, until they are low enough to truly observe. For five miles, they shadow the vessel, riding the air with such ease that they seem almost to float. Below, the boat's engine hums, but the Gulltides are silent, their focus unbroken.

As they circle the boat, their keen eyes scrutinise every detail—the glint of sunlight on metal, the steady movements of the rangers within. There is a spark of curiosity in their gaze, a flicker of ancient instinct driving them to understand this strange craft and its human occupants. The female Gulltide dives with precision, launching a series of swift water gun assaults that bewilder the rangers. Amidst the commotion, her partner seizes the moment to grab what he can.

In this orchestrated chaos, the female Gulltide spots an additional prize: a protein bar, rich with 400 calories. Unbeknownst to her, this clever choice will not only provide an extra source of nourishment but will also subtly enhance the pair's vitality, increasing their overall energy by 5%.

With their bounty secured, the duo soars to a secluded islet, a rocky sanctuary amid the shimmering sea. There, they feast on the beef and tomato bap—a substantial 660-calorie meal—and the protein bar, savouring their ill-gotten gains.

This remarkable adaptability to human offerings underscores the Gulltides' burgeoning presence in urban areas. By capitalising on our discarded provisions, they have seamlessly integrated into our world, thriving on the abundance we inadvertently provide.

With the man-made feast now a distant memory and hunger once again gnawing at their beaks, the pair of Gulltide set out on a relentless hunt. They take to the sea around the islet, circling in a sweeping three-mile arc, their wings beating tirelessly beneath the blazing late-afternoon sun. For hours, they dive and fish with determined precision, their eyes scanning the sparkling waters for signs of prey.

As the sun begins its descent, casting a warm glow across the ocean, their tireless foraging finally pays off. By the time twilight casts its veil, they have consumed an impressive bounty: krill, Mackerlure, and an elusive Glacisurge. This rare fish, part of the ice-type Animara class, is exceptionally rich in fat and calories. In total, their meal exceeds 1000 calories, providing the vital energy needed to sustain their vigour through the evening's encroaching chill.

With their bellies full and the sky darkening, the pair of Gulltide embark on a twelve-mile journey inland in search of respite. The taxing flight, a result of their exhaustive day of fishing and diving, leaves them weary. Using the remnants of warm air currents, they glide gracefully towards the shoreline, their wings outstretched to conserve energy. As twilight settles, they alight on a small, secluded rocky outcrop, seeking solace for the night. Yet, above them, a silent observer watches intently from a huge dune, the darkness concealing its presence but not its intent.

Under the moon's watchful gaze, the moonlit beach and grassy dunes are alive with tension. A Toxipurr, a rare and endangered Dark Poison Type Animara measuring around fifty-two centimetres from nose to tail, moves with predatory grace. Its sleek, shadowy coat blends seamlessly with the dim sands as it tracks a pair of Gulltides.

A nearby Animara spots the feline hunter and emits a piercing cry of terror. This alarmed cry jolts the Gulltides into a frantic panic. Their once peaceful roost erupts into chaos as they leap into the air, wings flapping wildly. The Toxipurr reacts instantly, pouncing with explosive speed. Its jaws snap shut around a few tail feathers in a brief, fleeting victory. However, the Gulltides, driven by instinct, manage to evade the Toxipurr's grasp. With powerful wingbeats, they soar away into the night sky, escaping back to the safety of the open sea.Frustrated yet undeterred, the Toxipurr resumes its relentless pursuit. It lowers its head and picks up another scent, its determination unwavering. The hunt continues beneath the moonlit sky, in the unyielding cycle of predator and prey.

Chapter Nine: The Hunter in the Shadows

In the quiet embrace of the night, the two Gulltides glide low over the moonlit ocean, their feathers gently ruffled by the cool sea breeze. Having narrowly escaped the clutches of the relentless Toxipurr, they now search urgently for a haven.

The rich scent of fruit on the wind reaches their acute senses. While both Gulltides have a keen sense of smell, the female's abilities are especially remarkable, particularly as she nears the breeding season. Her extraordinary olfactory prowess allows her to detect the faintest whiff of food from miles away.

Tonight, her heightened senses pick up the sweet, enticing aroma that drifts across the ocean. With a swift, instinctive turn, she leads the pair eastward, guided by the promise of nourishment and safety. The moonlight unveils a lush island, its fruit-laden trees gleaming in the soft, silvery glow.

As they approach, the island reveals itself as a verdant paradise, bursting with ripe, succulent fruit. With a sense of relief and newfound tranquillity, the Gulltides descend towards the island.

They find a particularly suitable tree, its branches heavy with the bountiful fruit they had been seeking. Settling into the lush foliage, they prepare to rest for the night, finding comfort and safety amidst the abundant fruit. Here, in this serene and fruitful sanctuary, they can finally relax, their earlier fears and exhaustion melting away under the gentle light of the moon.

As dawn gently illuminates the small island of plenty, the soft, melodious calls of morning birds fill the air, heralding a new day. Awakened by these tranquil sounds, the Gulltides are greeted by a sensory feast; the vibrant sight and intoxicating aroma of their surroundings bring them immense joy. Before them lies a paradise of Evolis fruit; these unripe, stone fruit are brimming with a staggering 800 calories. As they begin their feast, the island's bounty promises a day of unrivalled abundance.

As the Gulltides rest by the lake, they are soon joined by a variety of other Animara drawn to this essential watering hole. The tranquil waters invite a diverse assembly of creatures—an Otterling dips its snout into the cool surface, while a pair of shimmering Fenling's flit gracefully among the reeds.

The lake's serene ambiance is further enhanced by the arrival of a gentle giant. The Boartusk approaches the water's edge with measured steps, its massive frame stirring the lake's surface with each movement. The lake, serving as a vital oasis, becomes a harmonious gathering place where these diverse inhabitants share in the life-giving bounty and peaceful refuge it offers.

At the water's edge, the female Gulltide takes a refreshing bath, her feathers glistening as she mingles with the grass and water-type Animara. Meanwhile, our tagged Gulltide enjoys a spot of gentle fishing, skillfully catching a small fish Animara that yields 200 calories, a perfect addition to its already abundant morning.

In the gentle glow of the morning, the male Gulltide returns to his partner at the lakeside, where the two reunite with soft calls of recognition. Their bond, ever growing, is reaffirmed as they engage in a tender session of mutual preening. Each careful stroke of the feather is a gesture of trust and affection, reinforcing the connection they share. With their ritual complete, the pair takes to the skies once more, wings beating in perfect harmony. Together, they soar above the tranquil waters, their flight a testament to the enduring bond that guides them through the challenges of the wild.

With renewed vigour, the two Gulltides ascend into the sky, their bellies full and their spirits high. Their wings slice through the crisp air as they embark on one final foraging flight over the lush island before beginning their journey northeast, towards the distant breeding grounds. The landscape below, a tapestry of green, stretches out endlessly as they skim the treetops.

The female Gulltide veers sharply, her keen eyes locked onto something below. With a swift, graceful dive, she takes the lead, as if following some ancient, unseen trail. Her partner instinctively follows, the pair now moving in perfect synchrony. It is as if the very earth itself whispers to her, guiding them toward a hidden prize. This moment, charged with purpose and instinct, reveals the Gulltides' remarkable ability to navigate and adapt, driven by the eternal rhythms of nature.

In a sudden and graceful descent, the female Gulltide plunges toward the ground, her wings adjusting with precision as she levels just above the earth.

Her partner, caught off guard, follows closely, his movements a fraction less fluid but no less determined. She leads him along a narrow stream, its waters glinting in the dappled sunlight, the gentle trickle barely audible over the beating of their wings.

With every twist and turn, the landscape becomes more mysterious, the trees growing denser and the air cooler. As they continue, a veil of mist rises, shrouding the path ahead in an ethereal glow.

Undeterred, the female Gulltide slows her pace, guiding them deeper into this hidden realm. Her instincts are sharp, each movement deliberate, as if drawn by some ancient memory encoded in her very being. The pair ventures on, the mist wrapping around them like a cloak of secrecy.

What the Gulltides have flown into is, in fact, a Relict Forest—a surviving remnant of a once-vast boreal woodland that dominated this island centuries ago. Now reduced to a mere pocket, this forest stands as a living testament to a bygone era. Such relict areas persist where conditions remain favourable for boreal species, sheltered by cool, shaded valleys and fed by freshwater streams that maintain the moisture levels crucial for these ancient trees and plants.

The dense canopy protects the forest floor from the harsher sun, preserving the cool temperatures needed for its inhabitants. Within this secluded habitat, shrouded in mist, lies a secret.

The Relict Forest hides a rare and mythical creature, the Nautilix, who quietly thrives. This Water Dragon-type Animara, reminiscent of the legendary Dragonair, weaves gracefully through the forest's crystal-clear streams. With its sinuous, serpentine body adorned in shimmering azure scales, the Nautilix moves like a living ribbon of light, its long, elegant fins undulating softly with each motion. Its luminous, gem-like eyes, full of ancient wisdom, observe the world with calm curiosity.

Nearby, the Gulltides forage along the stream's edge, their attention fixed on the forest's abundant offerings. Oblivious to the gentle presence nearby, they are unaware of the docile Nautilix that watches them with keen interest. The Relict Forest, with its ancient trees and hidden waters, remains a sanctuary for these enchanting beings, preserving the magic of a world where ancient and wondrous creatures still dwell in harmony.

Despite its rarity, the Nautilix is renowned for its remarkable curiosity and desire to forge connections. As this elusive Water Dragon approaches, it draws closer to the pair of Gulltides foraging along the stream's edge.

The male Gulltide, ever vigilant, detects the shimmering movement in the water and tenses, preparing to protect his partner. His mate, noticing the glint as well, becomes equally alert.

However, the Nautilix's intentions are peaceful. With a graceful, dragon-like demeanour, it emerges from the water bearing a thoughtful gift. Balanced delicately in its elegant jaw are four ripe Evolis fruits. The Nautilix places these fruits beside the winged Animara and nudges them forward, extending an offering of friendship.

The Gulltide couple, recognizing the gesture, respond with a harmonious chirp and a respectful bow. They accept the gift with evident warmth, marking a moment of serene and genuine connection in the heart of the Relict Forest.

As night envelops the Relict Forest, the three Animara—Nautilix, and the Gulltide pair—savour the generous bounty of the Evolis fruits. The fruits, each packed with an astonishing 1,000 calories, nourish them deeply, their rich, sweet flavours enhancing their shared moment.

In a tamed setting, such fruits would be a vital part of training, aiding in the evolution of Animara. Yet here, in this serene moment, their purpose is even grander: strengthening the bond between the Gulltides and their new friend.

As the moonlight filters gently through the misty canopy, casting a silver glow upon the stream, the trio settles comfortably by the water's edge. The tranquil night settles around them, marking the beginning of a profound friendship forged under the stars, as they drift into restful slumber together.

As the first light of dawn begins to spread across the tranquil home of the Nautilix, the three slumbering Animara remain blissfully unaware of a lurking threat. Hidden in the shadows, a Toxipurr prowls with careful intent, having tracked its prey over land and sea with unwavering determination. This cunning predator moves stealthily through the underbrush, its gaze fixed on the unsuspecting group. The serene scene, bathed in the gentle light of the new day, contrasts sharply with the silent menace that draws ever closer, preparing to disrupt the calm of this idyllic moment.

Chapter Ten: Between Two Worlds

With predatory stealth, the Toxipurr springs from the undergrowth and in a sudden clash of wild forces, the serenity of the Relict Forest erupts into chaos. Its venomous fangs sink into the female Gulltide, who thrashes in panic, wings flapping erratically.

Seeing his partner in peril, the male Gulltide, driven by fierce protectiveness, takes to the air with swift agility. He launches a series of intense Water Gun attacks, each stream of water blasting towards the Toxipurr with impressive force.

The Toxipurr, however, remains undeterred, its fierce resolve pushing it through the assault. The battle intensifies as the Toxipurr retaliates with a relentless spray of needle-like darts from its tail, each one puncturing the air and striking the Nautilix.

The dragon, glowing with an ethereal aura, endures the painful onslaught. As the male Gulltide continues to bombard the Toxipurr with Water Gun attacks, the Nautilix shifts to an impressive aerial manoeuvre. He dives in with a powerful Quick Attack, further disrupting the Toxipurr's assault. With a surge of determination, the Nautilix, now glowing brilliantly, swings its serpentine body and delivers a decisive blow, freeing the female Gulltide. As the male Gulltide rushes to her side, the Nautilix fires a dazzling Opal Beam, encasing the Toxipurr in a gleaming block of ice. The forest falls silent, the battle's outcome sealing their triumph and restoring peace to the once-tranquil haven.

As the tumultuous clash subsides, the ever-graceful Nautilix turns its attention to the poisoned female Gulltide, gently lifting her onto its sleek, serpentine body. With serene precision, it glides through the clear waters, carrying her to a small, flat rock nestled further upstream. Here, the true majesty of the Nautilix is revealed, showcasing its legendary status among Animara Trainers and champions alike. Surrounded by a misty shroud, the Nautilix performs a spectacular feat.

It emits a radiant, crystal-blue beam that slices through the mist, creating a shimmering aperture high above. As the fog particles mingle with the mist, they descend like a restorative rain, healing and revitalising all they touch. This rare move, known as Dragon's Wish, not only heals but grants a profound wish to each restored Animara, fulfilling their deepest desires. Witnessed only a few dozen times in recent years, Dragon's Wish is a breathtaking testament to the extraordinary powers of these majestic beings.

It is a profound mystery, the nature of the Nautilixs' heart. Often regarded as simple creatures with limited self-awareness, they demonstrate a remarkable depth of compassion that transcends their type, class, and region. Their unwavering empathy and genuine care for one another reveal a level of emotional richness that far exceeds our human interactions. This boundless kindness and the strong bonds they form with their fellow Animara challenge our assumptions and offer a model of connection and loyalty we struggle to emulate.

If only we, as humans, could mirror such universal compassion and forge connections that sweep across our divisions, how might it transform our relationships and deepen the bonds between us? The world of Animara offers a poignant reflection on the nature of empathy, inviting us to aspire to greater harmony and understanding in our own lives.

As the mist reforms and a fresh blanket settles once again over this serene sanctuary, the trio of Animara sense that their time together is drawing to a close. In the world of these enigmatic creatures, some behaviours hint at their unique ways of saying hello and goodbye, and this moment is no exception.

The pair of loving Gulltides, their feathers ruffled by the gentle breeze, chirp in harmonious unison. In response, the Nautilix moves with a series of rhythmic undulations, as if acknowledging their farewell in its own graceful language. Though the intricacies of Animara behaviour remain largely mysterious, our understanding suggests that this parting is not final.

Research into their social bonds indicates a strong likelihood that these three will cross paths again, maintaining a deep, enduring friendship throughout their lives. The world of Animara is indeed a realm of profound, and often inscrutable connections, yet the bonds they form are clearly lasting and significant.

As the final farewells are exchanged and bonds reaffirmed, our two Gulltides ascend into the sky, their departure marking a poignant end to their visit. They navigate through the misty embrace of the sanctuary, heading back towards the lake. This ten-mile journey will occupy the remainder of the morning, but it is a flight they undertake with effortless grace.

The lake, with its serene waters and tranquil surroundings, offers a perfect respite before their next migration. After a well-deserved rest, they will continue their journey northward to the mating grounds, where they will once again take flight to continue their seasonal rituals.

Chapter Eleven: A Sanctuary in the Storm

As our tagged Gulltide glides back toward the lakeside, both the Gulltides' azure plumages begin to emit a soft, mysterious glow. This is no ordinary sight; it's the unmistakable sign that their vital bond level has been met. You can't help but wonder if this was the result and gift of the Dragon's Wish. This bond, essential to their survival, unites them in a connection that goes beyond simple companionship.

As they draw nearer to the water's edge, the glow intensifies, radiating like a beacon among the other Animara gathered there. It's as if their connection is not just seen but felt, a shimmering display that speaks to the depth of their unity.

With a synchronised leap, the pair launches into the sky, their wings moving in perfect harmony. As they climb higher, the glow of their plumage intensifies, growing brighter with every beat of their wings. They engage in Synchronized Soaring, tilting their wings at identical angles and catching the same rising thermals. Their glowing bodies leave trails of light in the sky, a luminous dance that weaves their paths together. The higher they ascend, the more radiant their glow becomes, until they are like twin stars spiralling through the heavens.

At the peak of their flight, their glow reaches its zenith, a brilliant display of their bond. Then, as they begin their descent, the glow slowly starts to fade, gently dimming as it is gradually absorbed back into their bodies. By the time they reach the ground, the light has almost completely vanished, leaving just a faint shimmer on their feathers. The glow has not disappeared, but has become part of them, a silent testament to the strength of their connection, now hidden within until the next time they take to the skies together. With their vital bond fulfilled, the majestic birds set forth on their winter flight with renewed determination, heading toward the sacred mating grounds. Though the chill of winter lingers, the warmer eastern winds almost mask its bite, creating a deceptive softness over the landscape below. Driven by an instinctual need and a profound sense of purpose, these resolute travellers soar through the sky with invigorated resolve, their synchronised migration a marvel of nature's enduring rhythms. As they traverse the subtly tempered winter sky, their journey reveals a grand spectacle of life's relentless cycles, showcasing the remarkable adaptability and resilience of these avian wanderers. Now, these pairs of Gulltide act as one in a deeply symbiotic and loving bond. From this moment forward, we shall take their combined stats into account; this new combined stat level will guide our observations until the end of their pilgrimage, reflecting their united strength and renewed commitment to their journey.

Animara Metrics			
BOND LEVEL NOW IN EFFECT (LEVEL 4)			
Name: Gulltide (Male) Scientific Name: Larus Aquatilis Height: 55cm (21.65 inches) Weight: 1,750 grams (3.86 pounds) Wingspan: 1.5 metres (4.92 feet)		Name: Gulltide (Female) Scientific Name: Larus Aquatilis Height: 47 cm (18.5 inches) Weight: 1,500 grams (3.31 pounds) Wingspan: 1.3 metres (4.27 feet)	
	Male	Female	Combined
Current HP Score	100%	100%	100%
Total Flight Time	24 Hours	27 Hours	51.56 Hours
Distance Travelled	70 Miles	80 Miles	150.5 Miles
Calories Consumed	950 Cal	1092.5 Cal	2,042.5 Cal
Current XP Score	3,626.2 XP	4,169.13 XP	7,795.33 XP
XP Needed For Next Level	2,719.4 XP	3,127.31 XP	5,846.71 XP

As we turn our gaze upon these two Gulltides, it becomes strikingly clear that their harmonious pairing is far more than a simple marvel of nature—it is the linchpin of their very survival. The impressive combined stats they exhibit are a living testament to the depth and strength of their bond, a bond that will guide and sustain them through the long, gruelling trek to the warmer waters of the North. This migration, fraught with peril and uncertainty, is a journey of life and endurance, a passage that only the strongest pairs can hope to survive.

Yet, it is in this profound partnership—a union forged not only through synchronised flight and mutual support, but also through the countless perils they have faced together—that's where their true power lies. These Gulltides have braved fierce coastal storms, escaped the relentless grasp of predators, and endured the harsh scarcity of winter's grip, all chronicled in the chapters of their shared journey.

Now, as they ride the tidal currents of the East, slowly making their way northward, their unity becomes a beacon of hope, guiding them to the sacred breeding grounds that await them. In these warmer seas, far removed from the dangers that once shadowed their path, they will secure the continuation of their species. This is the ultimate testament to the unbreakable bond that has carried them through so many trials and now leads them, together, to the sanctuary where new life will begin.

As the first rays of dawn stretch across the sky, the bonded Gulltides continue their flight, riding the coastal wind currents that guide them eastward. These birds, with their sleek, aerodynamic forms, are masters of energy conservation. Each tilt of their wings is a calculated effort to maintain effortless flight, preserving strength for what lies ahead. Below, a vast herd of Grazeleks—an electric-type Animara renowned for their immense numbers—grazes across the reserve's grassy plains. These enigmatic and powerful creatures generate a subtle yet potent electric charge as they move, their static-like energy crackling through the air. The sky above begins to darken in response, as the Grazeleks' energy interacts with the atmosphere, charging it like a vast, natural battery.

As the herd grazes, their combined energy gives birth to a formidable electrical storm, which forms over the easterly end of the reserve. The storm's ominous clouds gather, swirling with latent power, and soon, it will sweep westward across the entire landscape. The Gulltides, ever-sensitive to the nuances of their environment, sense the storm's brewing intensity. They understand that survival hinges on conserving every ounce of energy, for when the storm eventually strikes, they will need all their strength to navigate its ferocity. Whether they choose to fly through the heart of the tempest or seek refuge in the turbulent winds, their fate will depend on the energy they have so carefully preserved. As they glide along the coast, the Gulltides remain vigilant, instinctively preparing for the challenge that nature is about to unleash.

As the Gulltides approach their sacred mating grounds, their incredible feat of gliding a staggering sixty miles on the coastal currents stands as a testament to their meticulous energy conservation. Their triumph is short-lived. The storm, ignited by the electric discharge of the grazing Grazeleks below, erupts with a ferocious intensity. The once gentle coastal currents are now thrown into chaos, and the sky darkens with a brooding, crackling energy.

The Gulltides, with their wings straining against the winds, find themselves in a desperate struggle to maintain their course. The storm's rage intensifies, sending violent gusts that challenge their every move. Faced with a crucial decision, the birds must either seek refuge in the brief moments of calm or continue to press forward through the storm's relentless onslaught. As they make their choice, the first lightning bolts pierce the sky, striking the ground with blinding brilliance.

The Gulltides, undeterred, navigate through the tempest with unwavering determination, their every instinct and conserved strength devoted to overcoming the storm's fierce assault. In the face of nature's raw power, they forge ahead, their resolve illuminated by the storm's dramatic display, as they strive to reach the sanctuary that lies just beyond the storm's wrath.

Chapter Twelve: The Silent Watcher

Amidst the relentless fury of the lightning storm, the two bonded Gulltides find themselves in a desperate fight for survival. The storm, an unbridled tempest of crackling electricity and torrential rain, engulfs them with its wrath. Each lightning strike cleaves the sky with blinding brilliance, while the air hums with dangerous static electricity.

Battling fierce winds and stinging rain, the Gulltides navigate through this maelstrom with grim determination. The lightning's jagged fingers come perilously close, casting shadows of imminent doom over the struggling birds. Their once-impressive sixty-mile journey now feels like a distant memory, as their struggle to evade the storm has reduced their progress to a mere five miles.

In a desperate bid for refuge, the Gulltides skim just above the ground, threading their way around and through the massive herd of Grazeleks grazing below.

The Grazeleks, oblivious to the tempest overhead, are forced into uneasy movement by the birds' swift passage, their bodies generating electric static that further intensifies the storm. The Gulltides dart and weave among the herd, their feathers slick with rain, their muscles aching from the strain. Yet, driven by an indomitable will, they press on through the rain and wind, their eyes fixed on the sanctuary of their mating grounds, just beyond the storm's relentless grip.

As the Gulltides desperately skim the ground, weaving through the immense herd of Grazeleks, the younger members of the herd become increasingly irate. Disturbed by the persistent presence of the birds, these juveniles retaliate by launching small, crackling streams of electric sparks from their horned heads. The air sizzles with the electric bursts, narrowly missing the Gulltides but illuminating the stormy landscape with dangerous brilliance.

In a bid to defend themselves, the male Gulltide attempts to fight back, releasing a pair of water gun-like streams from his beak. The jets of water momentarily deter the electric sparks, but they do little more than irritate the younger Grazeleks, who only intensify their efforts.

Despite the barrage of sparks and the relentless storm, the brave Gulltide pair presses on. The near-misses and the juvenile Grazeleks' counterattacks fuel their determination, driving them with renewed vigour through the tempest and the agitated herd, toward the safety of their mating grounds.

As the male Gulltide battles through the storm, a particularly intense stream of electric sparks from a juvenile Grazeleks finally connects, striking him with a jolt that reduces his health and XP levels by nearly 45% and a shocking hit that drops the males HP to just short of 35%, as indicated by his 'stat tag.' The male falters, struggling against the assault and the storm's fury.

Sensing her partner's distress, the female Gulltide breaks away from their tandem flight path, her protective instincts ignited. With fierce determination, she veers toward the offending Grazeleks, her wings slicing through the rain-lashed air.

 Circling the agitated juvenile, she provokes it into a frenzied chase, drawing it away from the herd. Seizing the opportunity, the female Gulltide manoeuvres to flank her target and launches a Wing Arrow attack. A volley of ice-cold arrows, like shards of winter's chill, erupts from her wings, striking the Grazelek's face with precision. The icy barrage halts the Grazelek in its tracks, providing the necessary reprieve for the male to attempt to recover, but it's not over yet.

In the midst of the storm, the female Gulltide hovers just a few feet from the Animara that dared to harm her mate, her eyes blazing with unbridled fury. Animara researchers have discovered that females of the Gulltide species enter a "lover's rage" once a deep bond has been formed with their mate. This intense connection triggers an instinctive, relentless attack whenever their partner is threatened. The assault only ends when the offender has either fled or fallen, ensuring the safety of their beloved mate. This rage is what we're about to witness. Amidst a roiling electric storm, nature's raw power is about to be unleashed.

The female Gulltide, her feathers bristling with a protective fury, hovers ominously above the battlefield. Below, the Grazelek, a young and defiant Electric-type, stands its ground, static energy crackling along its striped body as it prepares for battle. With a sharp, electrifying whinny, the Grazelek charges forward, unleashing a fierce Voltstrike.

Lightning arcs through the storm, aiming directly for the Gulltide. Driven by what researchers have aptly named a "lover's rage," she twists and dives with remarkable agility, evading the attack with a fluid grace honed by instinct and desperation.

Undeterred, the Gulltide retaliates. She harnesses the storm's moisture, forming it into a concentrated Aqua Burst, a swirling vortex of water that she releases with precision. The torrent crashes into the Grazelek, sending it skidding backwards across the rain-soaked ground. Momentarily dazed, the Grazelek shakes off the blow, its electric energy flaring once more as it prepares for a second assault. But the Gulltide, now fully consumed by her protective instinct, allows no respite. She ascends rapidly, wings cutting through the storm-laden air with fierce determination. At the peak of her ascent, she hovers, then dives with blistering speed, executing a devastating Skycleave. Her talons, charged with energy, slice through the storm, striking the Grazelek with unyielding force. The Grazelek collapses, unable to withstand the combined fury of the storm and the enraged Gulltide.

Victorious, she circles above, a vigilant guardian, having fiercely defended her mate in the heart of nature's most unforgiving elements. As the tempest wanes, the female Gulltide's fiercely protective rage gradually subsides, her resolve softening as the storm's fury recedes. With a final, vigilant glance at the fallen Grazelek, she gracefully descends to reunite with her mate. Together, the pair navigates cautiously through the storm's fading edges.

Their movements, though slower, reflect a shared determination as they make their way through the diminishing chaos. The lightning's brilliant flashes fade to distant rumbles, and the torrential downpour lightens to a gentle drizzle. As they press onward through the storm's remnants, their bond, reaffirmed through their ordeal, shines with renewed strength. The storm will soon head west, but for the Gulltides, their struggle is over, and they now emerge into the calm that follows, their ordeal behind them.

Although the storm has finally abated and the skies are clearing, the aftermath poses a significant challenge for the female Gulltide and her mate. The erratic wind currents and residual turbulence have rendered their original flight path almost impossible. As a result, they are forced to embark on an unwanted twenty-five-mile detour through rugged, rocky terrain that leads toward the volcanic northern regions, even as they aim for the warmer eastern coastline.

This unexpected diversion not only complicates their journey but also demands considerable energy, which is critically depleted after their battle with the storm. The extra distance and challenging terrain will exact a toll on their stamina, making it imperative for them to forage for food and replenish their energy reserves in the coming hours. Their survival now depends on their ability to regain much-needed calories to sustain their journey. With spring's first day just two days away, the urgency of their mission intensifies.

They must navigate northward until the winds stabilise, then correct their course eastward to reach their destination in time for the mating season. Every moment counts as they strive to overcome these new obstacles and fulfil nature's ancient rhythms.

Chapter Thirteen: The Struggle for Sustenance

In the heart of this geothermal haven, where volcanic and rocky forces converge, the heat and stress are palpable. Our pair of Water Flying Animara, the Gulltides, glide through the demanding borders of this fiery expanse, where geothermal vegetation thrives amidst the harsh conditions. The relentless heat, combined with the presence of Fire and Rock-type Animara, creates a taxing environment that has drained their energy reserves.

Each Gulltide has expended approximately 150 calories in their struggle through this relentless landscape. The very air seems to shimmer with heat, and the turbulent currents only add to their ordeal. Their only hope lies in ascending to higher altitudes, where cooler pockets of air offer a potential refuge. Here, they must seek respite from the oppressive heat and find the vital energy they need to continue their journey, navigating this harsh and unforgiving frontier.

As the Gulltides ascend on the thermal updrafts, the female's eyes remain vigilant and tenderly focused on her wounded mate. With each minute that passes, the blistering heat of the geothermal landscape fades behind them, replaced by the cool, soothing currents of higher altitudes. The pair glides effortlessly, the female gently nursing and guiding the male, her protective instincts driving her to ensure he finds relief and recovery. As they rise, the intense warmth gives way to a more temperate atmosphere, offering them a brief respite.

Following her sharp intuition, the female leads them down through the cooling air currents, manoeuvring skillfully through the rocky outcrops and venting heat. Their flight eventually brings them to a volcanic runoff, where the waters, cooled by recent rains and geothermal activity, form welcoming, temporary pools. Here, the weary couple finally finds solace. The female tenderly helps the male to drink and rest, their shared struggle giving way to a precious moment of recovery and renewal as they replenish the lost calories and regain their strength.

As the male Gulltide lies weakened by the storm's lightning, his devoted mate works tirelessly to aid him. In the harsh volcanic landscape, she hunts the fiery Pyrocaris, a resilient Fire/Bug-type Animara adapted to the intense heat. Each time she captures one, its searing embers singe her wings, causing her small, painful burns. Despite the discomfort, she persists, driven by an unwavering dedication to her mate.

Each Pyrocaris, providing around 15 calories, is offered to the male Gulltide, who gradually regains his strength. After delivering a total of 55 calories, the female finally pauses. Her own wounds and exhaustion compel her to seek nourishment, as she turns her attention to foraging for herself, having ensured her mate's recovery with her selfless efforts.

Amidst the volcanic landscape, the female Gulltide, having endured the burns from the fiery Pyrocaris, manages to collect enough of these hot-tempered insects to replenish around 25 calories. Her tenacity and care are palpable as she finally returns to her mate. After a session of tender mutual preening, their bond visibly strengthened by shared adversity, they take a much-needed rest.

As the evening settles, the warm geothermal pool provides a soothing refuge. The gentle hum of the geothermal vents fills the air as the pair nestles together, their weary bodies finding solace in the warmth. In this tranquil respite, surrounded by the soothing embrace of the geothermal heat, they settle into a peaceful slumber, the trials of the day gradually fading as evening draws in.

As evening settles over the geothermal landscape, the harsh glare of day melts into the soft, warm hues of twilight. The geothermal vents, which have hissed and steamed relentlessly, now release a gentler plume of steam that shimmers in the fading light. The volcanic terrain cools slightly, with steam rising languidly from the thermal pools, and the rocks, covered in mineral deposits, glisten in hues of orange and gold. In this serene setting, the female Gulltide, having replenished her strength, gently nudges her mate awake.

With a renewed sense of purpose, they take to the skies in perfect harmony, though the male struggles at times to keep pace. His wings falter slightly, betraying his earlier weakness. Nevertheless, the pair glides eastward, their movements synchronised, as the stars pierce the indigo sky. The bioluminescent flora below casts an ethereal glow on their path.

The transition from day to night enhances the enchantment of their journey. The volcanic landscape below transforms into a shimmering tapestry of cool blues and silvers. The gentle steam rising from the geothermal pools creates a soft, enveloping mist. The male, despite his intermittent struggle, draws strength from the rhythmic motion and the comforting presence of his mate. As they ascend, the cool air offers a refreshing contrast to the warmth below. Guided by the stars and the bioluminescent flora, the Gulltides press on, hopeful that by morning, they will reach their cherished mating grounds.

As the night deepens, the two Gulltides press eastward through the rugged geothermal landscape. The female, ever watchful, expertly guides them through the searing heat, deftly avoiding the scalding geysers and the fiery nocturnal Animara that lurk in the shadows. The male, though determined, struggles intermittently, his wings betraying the strain of his injuries.

Each time he falters, the female adjusts her pace, gently encouraging and supporting him with tender nudges. After covering twenty miles, the relentless heat of the northern vents begins to abate, giving way to the soothing warmth of the northeastern sea. As they approach, the distant whispers of other Gulltides drift on the wind, signalling their nearing destination. With renewed hope, the pair continue their steady journey, the female's unwavering care guiding them towards the mating grounds, just as dawn begins to break. After another ten miles of navigating the cool night air, the two Gulltides, their wings heavy with fatigue, finally succumbed to exhaustion. As the stars shimmer overhead, they descend gracefully to the ocean's surface. With a gentle splash, they land and float, their wings partially submerged. They make their way to a nearby sandy outcrop, a refuge from the relentless journey.

Here, amidst the soothing sound of gentle waves, they settle into the soft sand. As they rest, the rhythmic ebb and flow of the tide eases them into a well-earned slumber, marking a serene pause in their long voyage. As dawn breaks over the vast sandbank, the two bonded Gulltides stir from their rest, the need to forage sharp in their minds. The gentle rhythm of the tide accompanies their rising, but a far deeper instinct drives them—the urgent need to reach the mating grounds, now just miles away. However, their journey will be futile if they cannot attain the crucial "mating level." Though they have reached the age to breed, it is not age alone that ensures success. Their bond must reach a certain depth of strength, one recognized by the evolved form of their species—the noble Waveplumes.

In the eyes of the younger Gulltides, the Waveplumes are akin to royalty, standing as the grand protectors and gatekeepers of the mating grounds. Revered and admired, they hold the power to grant or withhold permission for mating, their presence commanding awe and respect. Only when the Waveplume couple—majestic and wise—deem a younger pair's bond strong enough will they allow the privilege of breeding. Foraging well together and living in harmony are essential, but the true test lies in forging an elemental connection deep enough to impress the Waveplumes.

Until this bond is recognized by the royal couple, the young Gulltides will remain on the outskirts, watching and waiting. To succeed, they must prove their worth, aligning their spirits with the ancient forces that govern their world. With the sun climbing higher, the Gulltides take to the skies, their wings slicing through the air with an elegant grace. They circle above their small island, the vast ocean below a shimmering tapestry of blue. As the warmer waters prompt an influx of migrating schools and other aquatic Animara, the sea becomes a bustling arena of life. The gulls' keen eyes scan the teeming waters, alert to every movement. As they spot a promising school of fish, the pair prepares for their synchronised plunge. With a precise tuck of their wings and a sharp, aerodynamic dive, they aim to pierce the surface with pinpoint accuracy, a hallmark of the Gulltides' hunting prowess.

Chapter Fourteen: Echoes of Instinct

As the sun reaches its zenith, the Gulltides face a critical decision. Their earlier dives into the waters yielded only a modest catch of krill, each providing a meagre 100 calories. Spotting promising activity three miles west, the bonded pair changes course with purpose.

Upon reaching a small string of islands, they join other Gulltide couples engaged in an intense feeding frenzy. From a height of about fifteen metres, the bonded gulls execute their dives with precision, folding their wings tightly to streamline their descent.

They pierce the water's surface with remarkable agility, emerging with the rare and calorie-rich Streamara, each providing 250 calories. They repeat this dramatic plunge four more times, their efforts rewarded with the vital nourishment they need.

In the tranquil aftermath of their aquatic feast, our intrepid pair of Gulltides embark on a new foraging adventure, spurred by a stroke of fortune. They set out on an impressive fifteen-mile journey across the ocean, their destination the towering nests of Nautilants—grand, rocky spires that rise dramatically from the sea like ancient sentinels. These colossal nests, home to the diminutive yet nutrient-rich Animara, promise a bountiful reward. The Gulltides are not alone in their quest; their companions from the earlier feast follow closely behind, eager to share in the abundance.

Upon reaching the nests, the Gulltides and their fellow foragers work in unison, launching a series of precise peck attacks to breach the fragile exteriors of these towering structures. Inside, the water-bug Animara is revealed, providing a substantial caloric boost. Each Nautilant offers 250 calories, with the queen yielding an impressive 500. The group efficiently consumes their fill, with the Gulltides devouring four of these treasures before their hunger is sated. Satisfied, the pair lead their companions to a nearby island. There, amidst the serene lushness of the island, the female Gulltide tenderly preens her male companion.

As she meticulously cleans his feathers, his wounds begin to heal and his strength is gradually restored. The rest of the group continues their feast, while our pair rests, rejuvenating in the calming embrace of their island sanctuary. With their energy replenished, they prepare for the final leg of their journey—the crucial flight to the mating grounds, where their future and the continuation of their lineage await. At this point, before the final flight to the mating grounds along the Eastern Coastline of the reserve, we shall check their combined stats, taking into account the Male Gulltide's recovery.

Combined Animara Metrics	
BOND LEVEL NOW IN EFFECT (LEVEL 4)	
Name: Gulltide (Male) Scientific Name: Larus Aquatilis Height: 55cm (21.65 inches) Weight: 1,750 grams (3.86 pounds) Wingspan: 1.5 metres (4.92 feet)	Name: Gulltide (Female) Scientific Name: Larus Aquatilis Height: 47 cm (18.5 inches) Weight: 1,500 grams (3.31 pounds) Wingspan: 1.3 metres (4.27 feet)
Combined HP Score	85%
Combined Total Flight Time	64 Hours
Combined Distance Travelled	190 Miles
Combined Calories Consumed	3.901 Cal
Combined Current XP Score	11,234 XP
Combined XP Needed	3,450 XP
System Notes	The male Gulltide's injury reduced flight time, distance, and calories by 30%, lowering combined stats. His gradual recovery improved HP, but the injury left the female's performance dominant overall.

Now, the time has come. The mating grounds, a mere ten miles east along the coastline, beckon our bonded Gulltides. As they glide effortlessly toward their goal, the trials of their journey—stormy skies, relentless winds, and lurking predators—fade into the past.

The mating grounds, nestled in a sweet spot between the moderate warmth of the East and the geothermal hot zone to the North, are now within reach. This final stretch—just ten miles along the coastline—marks the culmination of their sacred pilgrimage. Guided by ancient instincts and the salt-scented breeze, the Gulltides embark on the last leg of their journey toward a land of promise.

The waters here are perfect for their species, warmed by currents enriched with minerals from the geothermal vents, creating an ideal environment for courtship and nesting. As they near these sheltered shores, they are no longer alone. Other bonded Gulltides begin to converge from all directions, forming a small but growing flock, each pair united by the same ancient call. Together, they will soon touch down on this harmonious coastline, where land, sea, and sky meet in perfect balance. Amidst the safety of the flock, courtship displays will begin, and the Gulltides will fulfil their instinctual role.

Here, life renews itself, and their legacy endures in this wild, perfect corner of the Earth. One of the many fascinating mysteries of all Animara is their complex social structures, and this is no different for the Gulltides. As our bonded pair joins the newly forming flock, a remarkable dynamic begins to unfold. At the heart of the flock is the lead pair, more advanced in their evolutionary journey, standing closer to the elusive level 10, which requires 33,750 XP.

What's truly extraordinary is that this pair shares 15% of their bonded experience with the others—a generous exchange that benefits the entire group. This sharing of XP strengthens the flock as a whole, allowing the less experienced pairs to grow and develop at a faster pace. The closer the lead pair edges toward level 10, the more significant their contribution becomes, uplifting all those around them.

It is a living testament to the power of cooperation in the wild, where survival and progress are intricately woven into the fabric of the community. After a single hour of tireless flight, the Gulltide flock finally catches sight of their long-sought mating grounds. As the sun dips towards the horizon, casting a resplendent golden hue over the shimmering waters below, the culmination of one grand journey heralds the dawn of another. The high-altitude currents that have sustained them now gently guide their majestic descent, painting the sky with a breathtaking display of synchronised grace.

Rather than descending immediately to their nesting sites, the bonded pairs begin to separate from the main group, gliding softly toward the shoreline. This moment is a harmonious dance of hope and preparation, as each pair moves with serene purpose, their actions a testament to their anticipation and readiness for the next chapter of their lives.

Yet, the waters below remain out of reach. The flock must now await the arrival of the Waveplume couple, the most exalted figures within the Gulltide community, and the closest embodiment of leadership within the reserve. This illustrious pair, draped in regal plumage, embodies both the evolved attributes and the revered authority necessary to oversee the sacred rites of nesting and breeding.

As the pairs hover in poised expectation, the air is charged with a palpable sense of anticipation. The arrival of the Waveplume couple will signal the commencement of a new era—a chapter imbued with promise and renewal. With their noble blessing, the Gulltide will soon undertake the meticulous task of nest-building, ensuring the continuation of their storied lineage.

In this brief yet profound interlude, the flock stands on the brink of transformation. They are not merely waiting; they are preparing to embrace the promise of new life, ready to embark on a journey of creation and continuity. With each passing moment, they draw nearer to the fulfilment of their dreams and the enduring legacy of their kind.

In a remarkable display of avian social intricacy, researchers have uncovered that the Gulltides are, to date, the only known bird species to present gifts of food to their alpha couple. This extraordinary behaviour unfolds in the sacred ritual of nest-building.

As a gesture of gratitude for the coveted permission to establish their nests, the Gulltides offer a portion of their hard-earned food to the revered alpha couple. This act of generosity is not merely a token of thanks, but a profound ritual of reciprocity.

In the event that their request for nesting rights is denied, this food transforms into a poignant compensation gift—a final meal for the hopeful pair as they are gently escorted away from the mating grounds. This unique behaviour highlights the Gulltides' deep sense of respect and the intricate social bonds that define their community, adding yet another layer to the rich tapestry of avian life.

In the heart of the mating grounds, where the sun's golden light casts long shadows, the Gulltide couple we've been following faces an arduous challenge. As the once-abundant resources become increasingly scarce, their quest to find the perfect gift of food becomes a desperate race against time. With each passing hour, more hopeful Gulltide flocks and bonded pairs descend upon the same shores, further depleting the dwindling foraging opportunities.

The couple's search for a worthy offering—an act of gratitude that could sway the alpha couple's decision—turns into a test of endurance and resourcefulness. As they navigate the crowded and competitive landscape, their every effort is underscored by a palpable tension, reflecting the broader struggle for survival and acceptance.

Chapter Fifteen: A Gathering of Wings

Against the backdrop of a sprawling coastal reserve, our Gulltide pair embarks on a daunting aerial quest. Soaring high above the vast sea of their kin, their keen eyes scan the five-mile stretch of coastline and adjacent wetlands, now teeming with hopeful contenders. The odds are steep; resources are scarce, and competition is fierce.

As the pair completes nearly a dozen meticulous flyovers, they navigate this bustling tapestry of feathers and calls, each couple in search of the perfect gift—a gesture that could mean the difference between acceptance and rejection. Their efforts are a testament to resilience and determination, for every pass reveals the growing number of rivals and the diminishing availability of suitable offerings.

Our Gulltide pair extends their search far beyond the boundaries of the familiar mating grounds, journeying an impressive fifteen miles northward. Their quest for the perfect gift drives them into uncharted territory, leading them to a remote chain of islands emerging from the sea mist. Each island, blanketed in dense, verdant vegetation, teems with vibrant life—a lush haven of flora and fauna.

As the pair navigates these unspoiled isles, their sharp eyes scan the thriving undergrowth and bustling shores, seeking out the elusive offering that could secure their place among the elite. The islands present both an opportunity and a challenge, with their rich resources hidden amidst the dense foliage.

This extraordinary journey highlights the lengths to which these remarkable birds will go, driven by the hope of finding the perfect gift in their relentless pursuit of acceptance and survival.

In a bold and daring manoeuvre, our Gulltide pair ventures a remarkable fifteen miles from the familiar mating grounds, driven by their quest for the perfect gift. Their journey takes them to a remote chain of islands, where dense, verdant vegetation teems with life. After an hour of searching through the rich tapestry of flora and fauna, the male's keen eyes lock onto a sight both familiar and promising: two large, ripe Evolis fruits hanging temptingly from a branch.

The discovery fills the pair with renewed hope, as these fruits could very well be the key to securing their place among the nesting pairs. With a sense of urgency, they swoop down and grab the heavy fruits in their beaks, pivoting sharply in the air despite the strain of their load. The fifteen-mile flight back to the mating grounds now seems daunting, as the weight of the fruit makes every wingbeat more challenging. Yet, driven by instinct and determination, they push forward, knowing that this burden may be the key to their survival and success. But this prize has brought with it another, more dangerous problem.

The discovery has not gone unnoticed, and now, other Gulltide pairs, equally desperate for an edge in the mating season, begin to circle. What was once a solitary flight has transformed into a tense aerial dogfight—a test of skill and strategy. The rival pairs swoop and dive, attempting to snatch the precious fruit, hoping to offer it themselves and secure their place in the mating grounds. The air is alive with sharp cries and rapid wing beats as our pair expertly twist and turn, evading their competitors with remarkable precision. It's a contest of agility and endurance, with each bird pushing their limits. Yet, in this extraordinary spectacle of nature, it is less a battle and more a game—a high-stakes race back to the mating grounds, where only the cleverest and swiftest will emerge victorious, earning their chance to secure a future for their lineage. In the intricate ballet of seagull competition, a rare and prized catch ignites a dramatic aerial contest. Picture a devoted pair of seagulls, their beaks tightly clutching a coveted fruit, embarking on a high-stakes journey back to their mating grounds.

As they ascend into the sky, their route becomes a stage for a fierce spectacle of nature's own design. The air is soon filled with rival gulls, each pair eager to claim the prize for themselves. Their tactics are a display of ingenuity: water shots, sharp sprays of seawater, are launched to disorient and disrupt, while wing slashes, swift and calculated, aim to wrest the precious fruit from its holders. These encounters are not intended to harm, but to outwit and outmanoeuvre.

What is a straightforward fifteen-mile journey becomes, in reality, a gruelling thirty miles. The seagulls must navigate through a labyrinth of rapid climbs, daring dives, and strategic flanks. As they twist and turn through this aerial gauntlet, their competitors remain relentless, determined to seize their prize. Yet, through a symphony of expert navigation and resilience, the bonded pair manages to stay ahead. Finally, after a remarkable display of skill, they reach a secluded spot within the mating grounds.

Here, they find solace for the time being, having navigated their arduous journey with remarkable tenacity and finesse. As they settle into their secluded sanctuary, their paternal instincts surface. The pair begins constructing a small makeshift nest, as if the precious fruits they have secured are their future offspring, deserving of careful nurturing. This early onset of parental behaviour is believed to serve a dual purpose: preparing them for the responsibilities of parenthood and concealing their prize until the time is right. It is within this makeshift nest, cradling their hard-earned fruit, that they will vigilantly wait and protect their treasure.

Each bonded pair carefully guards their precious offering, but it is the females who now stand vigilant, as if the offerings were their future eggs. They await the arrival of the legendary Waveplume couple, whose presence will signal the long-awaited permission to mate. It could be hours or even days before the Waveplumes arrive, but in the meantime, the male dutifully forages along the rocky shores. Ever attentive, he returns with a small oyster-like Anima known as Cryoclams.

Each one, gifted to his mate, offers 137 calories — a token of his devotion. It will take around 500 calories, 250 each, before they are nourished enough to mate. Only when she is well-fed does the male feed himself, their ritual of patience and sustenance inching them closer to their moment of union. As spring unfurls its first week over the Eastern Coastline, the tranquil skies are transformed by a surge of vibrant activity.

After a week of patient anticipation, our Gulltide couple, along with countless others, have settled into the mating grounds, their eagerness now palpable. This morning, the air is filled with an exuberant energy that mirrors the season's renewal. The normally serene coastline comes alive with a symphony of jubilant calls, each echoing across the mating grounds like an undulating wave of sound. In celebration, the Gulltides deploy their remarkable water gun-like abilities, creating stunning arches of water that cascade through the air, reminiscent of a ticker-tape parade made of shimmering liquid.

Each bird, from the newly arrived pairs to the seasoned residents, gazes skyward in unified wonder. Above, the majestic Waveplume couple makes their grand entrance, performing an awe-inspiring flyover that seems almost ceremonial. This breathtaking display, a fusion of light and water, evokes both wonder and festivity among the observers below. Yet, as the spectacle unfolds, a thread of concern lingers — will the esteemed Waveplumes accept the offerings and grant their blessing? As the promise of spring blossoms, the entire community holds its breath, suspended between the thrill of the moment and the anxious anticipation of what is to come.

As the first light of dawn graces the Eastern Coastline, all Gulltide eyes are drawn to the majestic flyover of the celebrated Waveplume pair. With effortless grace, they glide above the mating grounds, their powerful wings cutting through the crisp morning air. They finally alight upon a distinguished, elevated rocky platform, known among the Reserve Rangers as the Pinnacle Perch. This subtly commanding area, formed from a series of flat, weathered boulders, rises just a few metres above the surrounding terrain.

The stones, smoothed and polished by the relentless forces of nature, create a broad, stable surface that serves as the focal point for the Waveplume couple. From this unassuming height, they survey the bustling activities below with ease, their presence both commanding and seamlessly integrated into the environment. As the Gulltides look on in silent awe, a thread of concern lingers—will the revered pair grant their blessing to the hopeful multitude? The Pinnacle Perch, dignified and elegant, bears the weight of anticipation and hope in its understated grandeur.

	Combined Animara Metrics
	BOND LEVEL NOW IN EFFECT (LEVEL 4)
Name: Gulltide (Male) Scientific Name: Larus Aquatilis Height: 55cm (21.65 inches) Weight: 1,750 grams (3.86 pounds) Wingspan: 1.5 metres (4.92 feet)	Name: Gulltide (Female) Scientific Name: Larus Aquatilis Height: 47 cm (18.5 inches) Weight: 1,500 grams (3.31 pounds) Wingspan: 1.3 metres (4.27 feet)
Combined HP Score	85%
Combined Total Flight Time	64 Hours
Combined Distance Travelled	190 Miles
Combined Calories Consumed	3.901 Cal
Combined Current XP Score	11,234 XP
Combined XP Needed	3,450 XP
System Notes	The male Gulltide's injury reduced flight time, distance, and calories by 30%, lowering combined stats. His gradual recovery improved HP, but the injury left the female's performance dominant overall.

Chapter Sixteen: Chasing the Warmth

Along the rugged cliffs of the eastern coastline, the judging event is about to begin. This, some would argue, is one of the few rituals of the avian Animara that other species of Animara have taken and adapted as their own, be it land-based or aquatic in design.

Our bonded Gulltides watch intently as a dozen pairs of hopeful parents rise above the crashing waves, their white and grey feathers gleaming in the golden light of dusk. They circle the windswept Pinnacle Perch, in perfect formation.

The sound of the ocean fades as the flock moves in solemn, rhythmic flight, not a single pair daring to break this almost ceremonial path. Below them, the jagged rocks and surging tides seem a world away, as if time itself has paused for this sacred moment. Then, it happens—the male Waveplume, stationed proudly in the centre of the perch, releases three piercing, trilling calls that carry across the wind.

The signal.

At last, the first pair breaks from the circle, their wings catching the salty breeze as they descend toward their evolved leaders. The sea breeze tugs at their feathers as their talons gently touch the smooth, time-worn rock. For a moment, they remain poised, the gravity of the moment weighing upon them. In the male's beak, he carries a plump, ripe berry, its deep crimson hue glistening like a jewel. Beside him, the female clutches a small cluster of golden fruits, their bright, sunlit skin a vivid contrast to the rugged stone of the perch. With deliberate care, they place their offerings before the Alpha Pair of Waveplumes on the time-worn rock. The leaders, perched high and watchful, regard the gifts with an inscrutable gaze. The tension in the air is palpable. The Gulltide pair stands motionless, their eyes fixed on the Alpha Pair, awaiting the decisive signal of acceptance or rejection. The male Waveplume, perched with an air of stern authority, fixes his discerning gaze on the offerings, his eyes calculating and sharp.

Meanwhile, the Alpha female examines each piece of fruit with meticulous care, her feathers slightly rustling as she scrutinises their quality. It's strange, but somehow, and unknown to Animara researchers, the male Waveplume possesses an uncanny ability to evaluate all Gulltide pairings with an accuracy that surpasses human technology. His keen eyes seem to scan the pair as if assessing their stats, XP, and move sets with an almost preternatural precision.

As the Alpha female completes her inspection, her gaze shifts to the mated pair, who stands nervously beneath them. The male Waveplume's intense scrutiny continues, measuring their worth with an almost tangible depth. At last, the Waveplumes reached a consensus. With a slow, dignified bow of their heads, they bestow their approval. Relief washes over the Gulltide couple as their place within the flock is secured. The surrounding flock responds with a gentle, approving chorus, their harmonious chirps affirming the couple's acceptance.

As the day slowly drifts towards evening, a palpable sense of tension blankets Pinnacle Perch. Our bonded pair, having weathered hours of anxious anticipation, finally takes to the skies. The setting sun bathes the rugged cliffs in a golden glow, as the pair joins the solemn procession of hopeful Gulltide, their wings beating in ceremonial unison around the revered perch and its Waveplume monarchs. Arriving at the tail end of the formation, they face a long, suspenseful wait before they can present their gifts and receive their judgement.

By this hour, only half of the reserve's Gulltide population has been judged and granted permission to breed. The rejected pairs, having faced the harsh reality of their unfulfilled hopes, have begun their solitary flights home. Their bonds, once vibrant and full of promise, are now severed as they return to their nests in silence, their hearts heavy with disappointment. As each Gulltide heads its own way, its silhouette fading into the twilight, it braces for the long wait until the journey begins anew next year.

For these pairs, the break in their bonds is a poignant reminder of the stakes involved and the fierce competition they must face again.

As our Gulltide pair continues their slow, ceremonial glide around the Pinnacle Perch, every beat of their wings carries the weight of their dreams and the gravity of their forthcoming judgement. The evening sky deepens, thick with the suspense of what is yet to come. At last, the moment arrives.

A charged tension grips the air, electric and expectant, as our bonded Gulltides break from the ceremonial flight path. They glide effortlessly on outstretched wings; the wind carrying them in a slow, spiralling descent toward the ancient Pinnacle Perch. Their feathers catch the fading light of dusk, gleaming as they cut through the cool evening air, riding the coastal updrafts with the grace of seasoned fliers. Below, another pair has just earned the coveted approval.

Now, with the cliffside bathed in the golden glow of sunset, our Gulltide pair touches down on the weathered stone, hearts pounding as they stand before the majestic Waveplume monarchs. In quiet reverence, they gently place the ripe Evolis fruit—protected with unwavering care—into the stone's shallow offering space. They step back with heads bowed low, wings spread wide in a display of humble submission, their respect unmistakable.

The Waveplumes, regal and commanding, begin their careful inspection. Their piercing eyes, honed by years of wisdom, scan the gifts and the Gulltides themselves with the precision of master appraisers. Every movement is slow and deliberate, as if the world itself has paused, waiting for the monarchs' judgement to be revealed.

Just as the male Waveplume begins his meticulous inspection, scanning the couple with almost supernatural precision, we too shall take a closer look. Using our own technology, we can check the stats of this pair, though even our advancements pale in comparison to the Waveplume's innate skill.

Animara Metrics Table			
BOND LEVEL NOW IN EFFECT (LEVEL 4)			
Name: Gulltide (Male) Scientific Name: Larus Aquatilis Height: 55cm (21.65 inches) Weight: 1,750 grams (3.86 pounds) Wingspan: 1.5 metres (4.92 feet)		Name: Gulltide (Female) Scientific Name: Larus Aquatilis Height: 47 cm (18.5 inches) Weight: 1,500 grams (3.31 pounds) Wingspan: 1.3 metres (4.27 feet)	
	Male	Female	Combined
Current HP Score	85%	100%	85%
Total Flight Time	30 Hours	34 Hours	64 Hours
Distance Travelled	90 Miles	100 Miles	190 Miles
Combined Calories Consumed	1,750 Cal	2,151 Cal	3,901 Cal
Current XP Score	3,650 XP	7,584 XP	11,234 XP
XP Needed For Next Level	LEVEL 5 REACHED	LEVEL 5 REACHED	LEVEL 5 REACHED
Combined System Notes	Level 5 is considered BREEDING LEVEL and has a cumulative effect on the overall stats of both Gulltides as such new stats will be added to the Metrics Table from this point on to cover both the 3-month mating season and the Gulltides 27 day pregnancy and incubation cycle.		

After what must feel like an eternity, the two elder Waveplumes—regal stewards of this ancient coastline—exchange a momentous glance.

Their eyes, imbued with the wisdom of many seasons, meet in a silent accord. With a dignified bow of their heads, they grant their blessing, an age-old symbol of acceptance into the revered courtship grounds. The tension that once gripped the air lifts, replaced by a profound sense of accomplishment and an uplifting promise for the future.

With hearts brimming with joy, our Gulltides they leap into the air with a burst of exuberance, their wings beating rhythmically as they ascend through the open, spiralling circle above—an aerial gateway to their new chapter. The sky, expansive and welcoming, envelops them as they emerge, their feathers glistening in the golden light of the setting sun.

They soar gracefully over the vast expanse of the mating grounds, their keen eyes searching the landscape below for the ideal spot for their nest. The rugged cliffs and shimmering waters below resonate with the promise of new beginnings. The once-quiet shore vibrates with the excitement of renewal, as the Gulltides embark on their journey to build their future, their success a hopeful affirmation of the enduring cycle of life in this remarkable coastal haven.

Chapter Seventeen: A Bond Forged in Flight

As the Gulltides glide over the sweeping expanse of their mating grounds, their eyes, sharp and discerning, survey the landscape in search of a prime nesting site. The journey, spanning three arduous miles, is both exhilarating and demanding.

Their once-promising prospects are now crowded; many of the best spots have already been claimed by other approved pairs, diligently weaving their nests into the rich tapestry of the coastline. The search brings a mix of anticipation and quiet frustration.

At last, their gaze settles on a salt marsh, a verdant fringe hugging the very edge of their designated grounds. Here, amid the undulating grasses and shimmering pools, lies a promising opportunity.

They descend with a graceful flutter to a hummock—a small, raised mound of soil and vegetation that stands resolutely above the surrounding marshland. This natural elevation, a precious find, offers both protection and strategic advantage. The hummock rises gently from the marsh, providing a safeguard against the encroaching tides that could otherwise threaten their precious eggs.

The salt marsh, with its rich, organic soils and dense vegetation, is an ideal nesting ground. Its proximity to abundant feeding areas ensures that the Gulltides will have easy access to vital nutrients. As they settle on the hummock, a sense of triumph and hope envelops them. Here, in the tranquil embrace of the marsh, they have found their sanctuary—a place where the rhythm of life will continue, nurtured by the gentle sway of grasses and the lull of the tide.

As the sun dips below the horizon, casting a dusky glow over the salt marsh, our bonded pair sets off on their nightly foraging flight. This salt-laden landscape, with its swaying reeds and briny air, is now their new home, where they will reside for the months ahead. Gliding over the water's edge, they search for food, calling to one another as they scout the terrain.

Nearby, other nesting pairs are doing the same, scattered across the marsh, yet never too far apart to hear the occasional cry. Each pair is focused on their task, gathering sustenance and strengthening their bond. These soft calls, carried on the wind, maintain a quiet connection between them, reminding the colony that while each nest stands alone, they are all part of a greater whole, watching over the safety of the flock as they settle into their new territory.

As twilight blankets the salt marsh, our diligent Gulltides have managed to gather a modest cache of around 80 calories from their evening foraging. Each berry and fruit they've collected is a small yet vital contribution to their nightly sustenance. This haul, though modest, will have to suffice until morning. For now, it represents a temporary respite in their relentless quest for energy. The real challenge, however, looms on the horizon.

With the first light of dawn, the true foraging will commence in earnest. The dawn will usher in a new phase of intense activity as the Gulltides must secure significantly more nourishment to meet the escalating demands of their roles. Each day will require a substantial intake of calories—about 250—to sustain their energy needs and provide for the developing eggs that will soon be part of their world. The energy they gather now is but a precursor to the greater effort required ahead. As night settles over their hummock, they prepare for the demanding journey that lies ahead, knowing that the real test of their endurance and resourcefulness is just beginning.

As dawn's gentle light spreads across the salt marsh, the Gulltide pair stirs from their slumber. The first rays of sunlight bathe them in a golden glow as they begin their morning ritual—an intimate, deliberate preening of each other's feathers. This quiet act, full of care and connection, strengthens their bond for the day ahead. In this fragile world, their partnership is vital.

Once their grooming is complete, they part ways, each drawn to their respective duties. The male, sharp-eyed and meticulous, takes to the air. His task is one of preparation—not only for the nest, but for something equally crucial.

As he glides over the marsh, his gaze sweeps the landscape, not just for nesting materials but for the perfect site to construct a cache. Just as the nest will cradle their future young, the cache will hold their sustenance. It requires the same careful attention: sturdy twigs to frame it, soft grasses to line it, and seaweed to conceal the precious stores within. Here, in the quiet recesses of the marsh, he will tuck away food for leaner days, ensuring the survival of their future brood.

The female also works with practised efficiency. Skimming over the marsh's surface, she expertly harvests fruits, seeds, and berries, swiftly returning each morsel to the nesting site. She piles them at the location of the yet-to-be-built nest—ready for the male to begin storing away when his cache is complete. Her task, immediate and nourishing, is as vital as his, ensuring there is food ready to store when the time comes.

In this delicate balance of roles, the Gulltide pair works in perfect harmony. The male builds, not just a home but a storehouse, while the female gathers her growing bounty beside the nest. Together, their efforts prepare them for the challenges ahead, ensuring that both nest and cache will safeguard the future in this ever-shifting, unpredictable world.

For the past hour, the male Gulltide has been diligently circling the nesting site, tracing a one-mile loop over the marshland below. Each lap is purposeful, his keen eyes searching for and collecting materials to construct his vital cache. With a tireless rhythm, he forages twigs from the surrounding reeds and mudflats, returning them to his chosen location—a secluded spot, ideal for discreet storage.

Here, he begins his meticulous construction, shaping the gathered twigs into a spherical structure, much like a nest but with a specific intent. The twigs are interwoven with precision to form a robust frame. Inside, he layers soft grasses to cushion and insulate, then adorns the exterior with seaweed to blend seamlessly into the marshland. As a final touch, he crafts a basic entrance—a small, camouflaged door made from overlapping twigs and grasses.

This covered entrance allows for easy access while keeping the cache secure from prying eyes. With the land-based cache nearing completion, the male's attention will soon turn to a nearby pool, where he will construct a similar cache beneath the water's surface. For now, however, his focus remains on perfecting the land cache.

After another half-hour of meticulous labour, the male Gulltide takes a moment to admire his work with a quiet sense of accomplishment. The land cache, now a perfectly shaped sphere of twigs, grasses, and seaweed stands complete, its entrance camouflaged and secure. He emits a distinctive call, a signal of triumph to his mate.

Understanding the message, the female swiftly takes to the air, her wings beating with a determined rhythm as she begins an intricate relay. She covers nearly three miles, first flying to the nesting site to assess the cache, then returning to the marsh waters to hunt for small fish, mussels, and other vital morsels. Her flight path is a graceful arc, each leg of the journey a precise effort to gather and deliver food. With every return, she deposits her finds into the cache, ensuring its readiness for the days ahead. This coordinated relay reflects their seamless partnership and their shared dedication in the ever-evolving landscape of the marsh.

With the land cache completed, the male Gulltide focuses on building the water-based cache, situated on a salt marsh. He selects a tranquil, shallow pool nearby, where the brackish water is ideal for preserving food.

The new cache will mirror the spherical design of the land cache but is tailored for its aquatic setting. He starts by shaping a frame of twigs, positioning it so that half of the sphere gently floats in the water while the other half rests on the marsh's soft, muddy bottom. To ensure stability and resilience, he reinforces the structure with reeds and grasses, which intertwine to provide a solid base. Inside, he lines the cache with a thick layer of water-resistant seaweed, offering both insulation and waterproofing. Additional seaweed is used to seal any gaps, keeping the interior fresh and protected.

Positioned about a hundred feet from the hummock where the nesting site is located, the buoyant sphere is now ready to be stocked with food, showcasing the male's careful craftsmanship and adaptability in the dynamic salt marsh environment.

Amidst the flurry of morning activity, an unexpected force of nature asserts itself. A majestic flock of Lumowlet, large electric avian Animara, soars gracefully overhead, their powerful wings beating in unison as they head westward. The sheer number and motion of these magnificent creatures conjure a rainstorm, a sweeping deluge that envelops the salt marsh. The once-bustling scene of the Gulltide pair's industrious nest building is now overtaken by the relentless downpour.

The storm persists long after the flock has disappeared from view. Rain pours steadily, washing away any hope of further progress on the nests. The Gulltide pair, their efforts momentarily thwarted, must now focus on a swift, determined task—transporting their precious food stores back to the caches, striving to keep them dry amidst the unyielding rainfall.

After a relentless thirty-minute relay, the Gulltide pair performs their vital task with remarkable speed and urgency. The male, moving with rapid precision, races the hundred feet to and from the dry cache, ensuring that their provisions are shielded from the encroaching storm. His haul includes dried seaweed, a medley of fruits, nuts, and berries, along with sun-dried crustaceans and insects. Each item is quickly stashed to maintain its freshness. Simultaneously, the female navigates the rain-soaked marsh with equal haste, securing small fresh fish, briny mussels, and moist, aquatic plants for the wet cache.

Though their stores are not yet complete, their frantic, synchronised efforts ensure that their provisions remain secure for now. The female has managed to gather about 200 calories in the wet cache, while the male has amassed approximately 800 calories in the dry one. Their swift, coordinated actions in the face of the storm's onslaught reflect their resilience and adaptability.

Chapter Eighteen: A Nest Among the Reeds

It has been two hours since the storm that ravaged the mating grounds subsided, leaving a sodden and silent world in its wake. The air, still heavy with the storm's humidity, seems to hold its breath, bracing for what comes next.

The Gulltides, their feathers weighed down by rain, huddle together in mutual comfort. With gentle precision, they preen each other, striving to dry their plumage and dispel the chill of the storm.

The female, though exhausted, takes to the sky with a determined beat of her wings, navigating the drenched landscape within a cautious three-mile radius of their nest. Each wingbeat reveals her concern—what new trials will she face as she searches for sustenance?

Below, the male shakes off the rain and ascends into the air. His task of gathering dry materials is fraught with uncertainty about what challenges lie ahead.

Together, despite the storm's aftermath, their unwavering resolve and shared purpose drive them forward into an uncertain future, their spirits buoyed by hope and resilience.

With a sense of purpose, he takes to the sky, his wings slicing through the damp air as he follows a determined flight path, always within earshot of his mate. For the next hour, he tirelessly collects materials from the marshland—dried reeds, driftwood, and resilient grasses scattered amidst the sodden terrain. Each piece is carefully clutched in his beak, his flight a rhythmic dance of retrieval and return.

Back at the hummock, he meticulously arranges the collected treasures. Laying a foundation of sturdy reeds and intertwined grasses, he weaves in fragments of driftwood and patches of moss, crafting a robust and insulating structure. Once his initial load is set, he ascends once more, his wings carrying him back to the marsh to search for more materials.

His ceaseless efforts speak to his unwavering dedication, each journey a crucial step in building a sanctuary that embodies hope and perseverance amid nature's relentless challenges. The male Gulltide exemplifies unyielding determination as he labours tirelessly to complete the nest.

What begins as hours of effort gradually extends into days, his relentless work culminating in a marvel of avian craftsmanship. The completed nest is physical proof of his dedication—a well-constructed fortress of reeds and moss, resilient against the elements and insulating against the chill. As he steps back to admire his creation, a profound sense of accomplishment radiates from him. This tireless endeavour, driven by instinct and hope, ensures a secure haven for the future, embodying the essence of perseverance amidst the raw forces of nature.

Meanwhile, the female Gulltide undertakes a relentless odyssey across the marshland, flying a circuitous route that spans up to six miles with each foraging trip. Her wings beat tirelessly as she navigates the drenched landscape, her beak harvesting an abundant array of sustenance. Over the course of her ceaseless flights, she amasses a remarkable 2000 calories, her diligent provisioning ensuring that both caches are well-stocked. This vital reserve will sustain them through the coming weeks, providing the necessary nourishment for the incubation period that lies ahead.

As the nest nears its completion, her foraging will naturally decrease, the occasional addition to their stores evidence of her tireless efforts. The harmonious interplay of his industrious nest-building and her exhaustive provisioning epitomises a profound partnership, their combined endeavours securing their future amidst the ever-present challenges of the natural world. In the delicate hush of twilight, as the final rays of the sun cast a golden hue over the meticulously crafted nest, the moment of truth arrives. With the intricate structure now complete, the female Gulltide steps forward. Her posture is poised, and her gaze, steady and assured, meets that of her partner.

In a graceful, almost imperceptible movement, she tilts her head and extends her wings in a subtle yet unmistakable display. This silent, elegant gesture is her way of conveying readiness—a signal as mysterious as the species itself. The male, recognizing the significance of her stance, responds with a soft, rapturous call, a sign of his own anticipation and readiness to embark on the next chapter of their shared journey.

In the stillness of their exchange, a profound understanding takes shape, marking the dawn of a new chapter in their lives. This moment, rich with significance, heralds the beginning of a period where their dedication and teamwork will be tested to their limits. As they prepare for the arrival of the new life that will emerge from their union, every glance and gesture becomes laden with meaning.

The communication between them is not merely a pause, but a deep, resonant acknowledgement of the journey ahead. It is a time of anticipation and preparation, where their bond will be put to the ultimate test.

Their commitment will be scrutinised as they ready themselves to nurture and protect the new life that is about to join their world. In this pivotal phase, each action will reflect their readiness to embrace the responsibilities and challenges that lie ahead, demonstrating their unwavering devotion and the strength of their partnership. This quiet moment, thus, is not just a transition, but a testament to their shared resolve and the future they are about to shape together.

Their interactions, imbued with a profound sense of intimacy, become increasingly tender. The female, with a delicate flutter of her wings and a soft, rhythmic coo, draws nearer to her partner. Each subtle movement—a nuzzle, a gentle preen—serves as an unspoken affirmation of their bond. The male responds in kind, his posture relaxed, yet attentive, as he edges closer, mirroring her quiet anticipation. Their shared glances and synchronised movements weave a tapestry of trust and affection. As they draw together, their mutual readiness culminates in a final, unspoken accord.

With our Gulltides on the cusp of mating, we shall grant them a moment of privacy. Spring is beginning to weave its magic over the salt marsh, slowly transforming the landscape. The air grows warmer, a gentle breeze rustling through the emerging shoots of grasses, while small clusters of flowers tentatively begin to bloom along the damp edges of the mating grounds.

Two weeks have passed since the Gulltides built their nest, and the season has now ushered in the act of mating. Nestled within the shelter of reeds are four delicate eggs, cradled beneath the devoted mother Gulltide. Her soft feathers, fluffed to form a protective blanket, warm her clutch as new life stirs beneath her. Meanwhile, the male Gulltide is foraging once more, the pair having consumed a remarkable 1000 calories in the last two weeks, now set out to replenish their dwindling food stores.

The marshlands, with the promise of new growth, offer berries, nuts, and fruits, but his focus remains on the vital calories needed—crustaceans and small fish. These rich sources of sustenance are what the pair need most during this critical time. With tireless effort, he scours the shallows and mudflats, seeking the nourishment that will sustain both his mate and their future offspring, as spring breathes life into the landscape around them.

Chapter Nineteen: Battling the Elements

As the male Gulltide glides effortlessly over the expansive salt marsh, his wings cut through the cool air with practised precision. Below him, the shimmering waters reflect the early spring of the reserve, where temperatures peak at around 10°C (50°F.). His keen eyes scan the tidal pools, attuned to the faintest ripple or flicker of movement.

He is on the hunt, searching for small fish, mussels, and crustaceans hidden within the salty shallows. Every motion is purposeful, his flight a delicate balance of grace and efficiency as he navigates the intricate ecosystem of the marsh, shaped by the tides and the cool coastal breeze. His foraging is essential, not just for his own survival, but for the nourishment of his mate and the future lives they guard.

Meanwhile, back at the nest, the female Gulltide remains steadfast, her watchful presence protecting four exquisite speckled eggs, ranging in size from 6cm to 7.5cm in length. These fragile treasures rest securely in a hollow of carefully arranged sea grass and feathers. With quiet grace, she adjusts her position, instinctively turning the eggs to ensure an even warmth—each movement critical for the delicate process of incubation. Now, with a sense of quiet pride, we pause to examine the health of both Gulltides—and, of course, their precious eggs.

After hours of steadfast incubation, the female Gulltide gently rises from her nest, allowing herself a brief moment of rest. She extends her wings, slowly unfurling them as if shaking off the weight of countless still hours. The muscles, long dormant, awaken as she stretches, easing the stiffness from her body. With quiet precision, she begins to preen, each stroke of her beak deliberate and meticulous. Her feathers, delicate yet strong, are tended to with great care, for they are her lifeline. They insulate her from the cold, protect her from the elements, and grant her the gift of flight. This ritual, far from mere vanity, is vital to her survival. Each feather must be perfectly aligned, every plume in its rightful place. Without this careful maintenance, she would be unable to face the challenges ahead—finding food, evading predators, and nurturing the next generation.

In this moment of quiet preparation, she readies herself for the trials of motherhood, ensuring that she remains a steadfast guardian of her future brood. In the grand tapestry of life, the temperature of an egg is a delicate thread that holds the promise of future generations. To cradle the future within, the egg must remain at a precise 37°C (98.6°F), an unyielding standard for its survival. As the temperature falls below this crucial mark, the egg's vitality (or HP on the stat tag system) begins to falter. Each degree of decline syphons away 5 HP, a stark reminder of nature's relentless challenges. The parent Gulltide, be it male or female, in its nurturing role, must diligently consume 200 calories each day. Should it fall short, the egg's warmth diminishes further, dropping 2°C for every 60 calories missed, thereby eroding the precious HP.

Nature's hand is also felt through the environment: temperatures plunging below 20°C (68°F) exact a toll, reducing the egg's HP by 2 HP each day. Conversely, warmth above 25°C (77°F) offers a reprieve, enhancing the egg's HP by 2 HP daily, but caution is paramount. Should the temperature soar above 39°C (102.2°F), the egg faces a 5% risk of failure for each additional day.

When the egg's HP dips below 20, the shadow of failure looms large, with a 25% chance of not hatching. If it reaches 0 HP, the promise of new life is extinguished. In this delicate interplay of warmth and nourishment, the future of life itself hangs precariously in the balance. The intricate equilibrium that sustains our world is both fragile and vital, proving the profound interconnectedness of all living things. It is in these tenuous conditions that the dawn of existence awaits, a promise shrouded in uncertainty. The fate of the four lives within the nest depends on the tender care their parents both extend, guiding them towards a hopeful future.

Thus, the future of life, poised on this fragile edge, yearns for the nurturing touch that will lead it to a new beginning. Each egg holds a fragile promise of life, and now, with the female momentarily away, we have the chance to check the vital statistics of these precious, developing young.

Animara Metrics Table				
BOND AND BREEDING LEVELS NOW IN EFFECT (LEVEL 4/5)				
Name: Gulltide (Male) Scientific Name: Larus Aquatilis Height: 55cm (21.65 inches) Weight: 1,750 grams (3.86 pounds)			Name: Gulltide (Female) Scientific Name: Larus Aquatilis Height: 47 cm (18.5 inches) Weight: 1,500 grams (3.31 pounds)	
	Male		Female	Combined
Current HP Score	85%		100%	85%
Total Flight Time	48 Hours		42 Hours	90 Hours
Distance Travelled	160 Miles		150 Miles	310 Miles
Combined Calories Consumed	2,350 Cal		2,250 Cal	4,600 Cal
Current XP Score	4,050 XP		7,8540 XP	11,900 XP
XP Needed For Next Level	10,950 XP		7,150 XP	3,766 XP
Nest Temp (°C) 34°C				Environment Temp (°C) 10°C
Egg Stats			Size (cm)	HP	XP
Egg 1 SizeXP and HP score			6 cm	50 HP	100 XP
Egg 2 Size XP and HP score			6.5 cm	68 HP	120 XP
Egg 3 Size XPand HP score			7.1 cm	80 HP	150 XP
Egg 4 Size XPand HP score			7.5 cm	70 HP	120 XP

In the tranquil expanse of the salt marsh, our male gull, still mending from his recent injuries, faces a daunting challenge. Despite the serene beauty of his new home, the toll on his wings has severely impacted his foraging abilities. Restricted by his condition, he ventures no farther than one mile from the nest in every direction. Within this limited range, he meticulously searches the surrounding streams and pools for high-calorie nourishment. This careful foraging is crucial, not only for his own recovery, but also for sustaining his partner and replenishing their vital food cache. Every cautious flight and meticulous search reflects his dedication and resilience, as he navigates the delicate balance between recovery and survival in this captivating landscape.

In the serene embrace of the salt marsh, our beleaguered male gull, restricted by the limitations of his recovering wings, remains close to the nest—a strategic choice that also keeps him within earshot of his partner's calls. As he diligently forages in a nearby pool, he stumbles upon a trio of mackerel, each brimming with 200 calories of life-sustaining energy. With measured efficiency, he consumes one, replenishing his strength, and carefully transports the remaining two back to the waterside cache, where they will await future consumption. As the strain on his wings intensifies, he makes his way back to the nest, greeted by a small chorus of welcoming calls from his partner. This tender exchange underscores the profound continued bond between them and highlights yet again the unyielding commitment to their shared survival, as each moment of care and cooperation weaves a story of resilience and devotion.

After an hour of rest within the nest, the female gull gracefully takes to the air, offering a small bow and chirping as a tender farewell to her partner. She departs, leaving the male gull to warm the eggs, which also allows him to recuperate from his earlier foraging efforts. Half an hour later, she returns, her flight purposeful and laden with a stalk of blueberries. Each of the six berries provides about 15 calories, totalling 90 calories. This nourishment will bolster both gulls' energy levels, highlighting their mutual care and resilience as they navigate the delicate balance of survival.

Chapter Twenty: Defenders of the Nest

As we return to our Gulltides halfway through the first week of the incubation period, a sense of tranquil progress pervades. The clutch of eggs, nestled with care, has shown a modest but encouraging increase in vitality. Both parents have taken turns tending to the eggs, their instinctual roles perfectly orchestrated.

The devoted mother now assumes the primary role, ensuring the eggs remain at the ideal temperature with each gentle adjustment. Meanwhile, the male Gulltide, having regained his strength to a commendable 95%, embarks on foraging expeditions with renewed vigour. His brief respite has restored his resilience, allowing him to venture further afield in search of sustenance.

As we follow the male Gulltide on his relentless quest, we find him at the most northerly point of their coastal mating grounds. His keen eyes scour the barren landscape, where every morsel has already been claimed by other mated pairs. Amidst this scarcity, a remarkable shift occurs in his behaviour.

No longer merely foraging, the gull's instincts turn to kleptoparasitism. In these lean times, he engages in a calculated pursuit of theft, targeting the caches of others and even snatching food from fellow gulls' beaks. Thankfully, near our Gulltides nest, food remains relatively accessible for now. However, as the competition intensifies and resources become scarcer, this fortunate situation may soon change. The male Gulltides' desperate measures highlight the harsh realities of survival in these coastal realms, where the struggle for sustenance drives both ingenuity and ruthlessness.

In the hush of dawn, as the sun casts a golden glow over the coastal expanse, our male Gulltide seizes a fleeting opportunity. With the nesting couple at the waterside fast asleep, their precious cache of mackerel—each brimming with roughly 200 calories—lies unguarded. Like a shadow in the early light, the male Gulltide swoops down with precision. A swift, calculated wing strike shatters the cache, and he plunges his beak into the nutrient-rich feast.

The seconds tick by like heartbeats as he hurriedly selects the most substantial morsels. His frantic movements stir the air, and the rising chaos soon awakens the nearby sleeping gulls. With three plump mackerels clutched firmly in his beak, he ascends skyward, the weight of his caloric bounty propelling him to safety. The raid was a stroke of luck, a brief but brilliant victory in the relentless battle for survival. Soon, he will share his spoils with his mate, but fortune is fickle—next time, he may not be so fortunate.

Back at the nest, the female Gulltide has momentarily stepped away to replenish her strength from the diminishing food cache. With a determined peck, she devours approximately 400 calories from the scant reserves, her actions underscoring the vital sustenance required to support her relentless duties. As she feeds, a subtle shift in atmospheric pressure and an imperceptible change in the wind's whisper catch her keen senses.

Although it is spring, a time usually marked by warming temperatures, coastal regions are not immune to sudden cold snaps. The once gentle breeze now stirs with a more pronounced chill, the biting winds only just beginning to coil and intensify. Her observant eyes detect a growing agitation among the nearby gulls, who hurriedly retreat into their nests. The air thickens with a palpable tension, signalling the approach of a cold snap rather than a full-blown storm.

This sudden chill, accompanied by the increasingly harsh winds, threatens to coat the eggs in frost and diminish the already scarce food supply. With instinctual precision, the female Gulltide braces herself against the impending cold, ready to shield her precious clutch from the encroaching frost that looms on the horizon. With its contraband securely locked in its beak, the male Gulltide embarks on the arduous journey back to its nest, a three-mile odyssey fraught with peril. At an altitude of around seven hundred metres above sea level, the once gentle breeze transformed into a relentless, biting gale—a true berserker of a cold snap. Each gust of wind slices through the air with a savage chill, further amplifying the challenge of the return flight.

The male Gulltide must navigate this frigidly high altitude, where the temperature's cruel grip reduces its XP gain by a staggering 10% every five minutes aloft. Despite the harsh conditions, the Gulltide presses on, driven by the primal need to deliver the precious cargo to their nest. The cold, unforgiving and unrelenting, tests its endurance and resolve, as every wingbeat becomes a battle against the icy onslaught of nature's wrath.

The cold snap has now been entrenched for two days, casting a frigid veil across the entire eastern coastline of the reserve. The temperature has plummeted to a harsh 3°C, well below the ideal for egg incubation. This sudden drop is starting to take its toll. With every 5°C drop below 20°C, the eggs lose 1°C of heat, putting their current temperature at around 28°C—dangerously far from the required 37°C. For each degree lost, the eggs lose 5 HP, making this cold snap a serious threat to their survival.

Despite their efforts to stay nourished, the Gulltides have only managed to consume around 400 calories between them, just enough to sustain themselves but insufficient to stabilise the eggs' conditions. Yet there is still hope. If the male can locate more calories soon, he may be able to buy precious time for his partner and their eggs, delaying the worst effects of the cold and giving them a chance to endure.

As the cold snap enters its third gruelling day, the male Gulltide once again takes flight, venturing two miles from the nest in search of food. The salt marsh below, though not entirely barren, is locked in winter's icy grip. The shallow pools are crusted with ice, and the mudflats, once teeming with life, are now quiet as creatures burrow deeper to escape the cold. Foraging has become a challenge, with much of the marsh's usual bounty hidden beneath frozen layers of earth. Above him, the skies are fraught with peril. Other Animara, equally desperate, circle the marshlands, their hunger driving them to vie for any scrap of food they can find. The male Gulltide dodges larger predators, his flight tense as he scours the frozen landscape below. His efforts yield only 100 calories, a pitiful amount compared to what is needed.

Of that, he consumes a mere 20, taking the rest back to his mate, knowing she must eat to protect their eggs. Weakened and battered by the freezing winds, he returns to the nest, knowing that time—and the cold—are against them. As night tightens its icy grip on the third day of the cold snap, the male Gulltide, already weakened by his fruitless search for food, feels the toll of the harsh conditions. Circling the frozen marshlands one final time, his wings struggle against the biting wind, his body growing heavier with each passing moment. He covers the fifteen miles around the nest, but the barren landscape yields nothing. With each futile dive, the cold saps his remaining strength.

By the time he returns to the nest, his health has plummeted by another 8%, and the unforgiving cold has drained his XP further, leaving him perilously low. His once powerful form is now shivering with exhaustion, his energy almost spent. With no food to offer, he settles next to his mate and their precious eggs. The cold gnaws at him relentlessly, but he presses close, sharing what little warmth he has left, desperate to keep them alive through the long, freezing night. Through the cold, unyielding night, the Gulltides huddle together, their feathers fluffed in a desperate attempt to shield themselves against the biting wind. The storm rages on, testing the endurance of these resilient birds, whose very survival now hangs in the balance.

Despite their efforts, the freezing air creeps into their nest, sapping the strength from their bodies. Health points fall, each parent losing 20% of their remaining vitality, while their precious stores of energy—measured in dwindling XP—slip away by 15%. Fatigue weighs heavily on their wings, leaving them weak and vulnerable in this harsh environment. Beneath them, the eggs are no longer safe. Their temperature has plummeted by 4°C, resting now at a dangerous 33°C, far below the necessary warmth for life to flourish. The smallest of the clutch, just 6 cm, is in the gravest danger. Its fragile shell, lacking the mass to retain heat, is now perilously close to the point of no return. In the silent hours of the night, the Gulltides can only wait helplessly, as the sheer cold continues to bear down, uncertain of the fate awaiting their young.

Chapter Twenty-One: Time is Cold and Fleeting

For four relentless days, an unseasonable cold snap has gripped the East Side of the reserve. Though it is the first week of spring, no warmth or sunlight has yet touched the frozen mating grounds.

The Gulltides, resilient as they are, huddle close to their eggs, their feathers fluffed against the biting cold. Alongside them, their evolved cousins, the Waveplumes, are engaged in the same desperate struggle—using every ounce of energy to shield their unhatched young from the icy onslaught.

Normally at this time of year, these creatures would be foraging along the shores, nurturing their eggs through the first week of spring. The parents would be steadily building up their caches of food, preparing for the busy months ahead. But now, their focus is singular: survival.

The starkness of this scene raises a crucial question—are we, as humans, contributing to these increasingly erratic weather patterns? The once predictable shifts in the seasons have given way to unsettling extremes, impacting not only the creatures here but Animara across the globe. Industrial emissions, habitat destruction, and climate change are no longer distant threats but immediate realities. As we witness the suffering of species such as the Gulltides, one must ask: how much of this disruption have we caused, and what does it mean for the delicate balance of nature we so often take for granted?

In the icy grip of the salt marsh, the Gulltides stir uneasily in their nest. Though they press close, feathers fluffed and bodies nestled together, the relentless cold invades, gnawing at their fragile warmth. The mother senses it first—something is wrong. One of the eggs, her smallest, feels far too cold beneath her. Her heart races with instinctive fear. With a few urgent chirps, her partner understands. Without hesitation, he launches into the freezing air, his wings heavy with the chill. Every gust of wind pushes against him, but he knows they need food—and fast.

Without the energy from precious calories, their eggs, already struggling, may not survive another day. Yet the biting cold has driven prey into hiding, and the male Gulltide fears the worst as he fights against the unyielding sky. Back at the nest, the mother turns her focus to the eggs. The smallest, a vulnerable 6.2 cm egg with only 50 HP, has dropped below 34°C, its health now hanging at a precarious 30 HP. The chill stiffens her wings and makes each movement a painful struggle. With every turn of the egg, she worries if her efforts will be enough. The fear gnaws at her as she fights to keep her precious offspring alive, knowing that without the warmth of food and her mate's return, time is running out.

For over an hour, the male Gulltide has circled tirelessly, keeping to a wide five-mile orbit around the frozen mating grounds. His keen eyes, though sharp, struggle against the biting wind and dense mist clinging to the salt marsh. Time is running out—his mate and their eggs grow colder with each passing minute. Then, through the haze, he spots it: a small fish darting beneath the surface. With a swift dive, he captures it, but before he can climb, another male Gulltide streaks through the air, wings cutting like knives.

The sky erupts into a furious dogfight. The rival Gulltide swoops in, beak snapping, wings flaring as they twist and turn, locked in a brutal aerial battle. Feathers fly as they slash and strike, each trying to outmanoeuvre the other. Beak meets wing, claws rake through the air, and in the chaos, both birds lose precious energy, each dropping 5HP with every desperate clash. The fish, caught in the fray, slips free, falling back into the marsh.

It's the fourth time today his hard-won meal has been stolen, and the male is weakening. With each fight, his strength dwindles, and the cold gnaws at his bones. But he can't stop. His family is waiting, the eggs on the edge of survival. He rises once more, scanning for a final chance. As the Gulltide glides above the rugged coastline, it scans the myriad rock pools and hidden inlets below. The gull's gaze sharpens with an intense focus.

Amidst the shifting sands and seaweed, something large and sluggish emerges from the briny depths—a solitary Canpagurus. As Canpagurus advances across the frostbitten salt marsh, its massive claws glint in the icy light. Suddenly, Gulltide swoops down, blocking Canpagurus's path with a determined glide, its wings spread wide in a desperate attempt to prevent the crustacean from retreating to the safety of the frigid sea. Despite its resolute stance, our Gulltide is sluggish, weakened by the harsh cold and low energy. The two adversaries face off in a tense stare-down.

Canpagurus, undeterred by the icy conditions, launches a powerful Claw Strike, the attack amplified by the frozen ground. Gulltide clumsily flaps to the side, its Water Blast barely registering due to the biting cold sapping its strength. Seizing the advantage, Canpagurus delivers a crushing Claw Crush, slamming into Gulltide and sending it spiralling through the air.

Exhausted and battered, Gulltide attempts a final Wind Surge, but the effort falls short. With a last, decisive blow, our tagged Gulltide knocks Canpagurus unconscious. In a remarkable turn of events, the battered gull who was now suffering with a mere 15% of its HP remaining is struggling but resolute. It manages to grasp the incapacitated crustacean in its talons.

Despite the cold and its injuries, the Gulltide takes flight, carrying Canpagurus back to its nest. There, the unconscious crustacean will become a vital meal for our Gulltide and its mate, ensuring their survival through the harsh, icy conditions of the salt marsh. As the hours drag on, our Gulltide battles through the frigid sky, its once-mighty wings now weary and burdened from the relentless five-mile trek to the nesting hummock. Every beat of its wings is a testament to its sheer determination. The weight of the unconscious Canpagurus, heavy and awkward, makes the journey even more gruelling. Navigating low over the cold, grey expanse of the salt marsh, the Gulltide carefully avoids any further confrontations, its energy dwindling with each passing minute. Finally, the faint silhouette of the nest emerges on the horizon, offering a glimmer of hope.

With a last surge of strength, our Gulltide ascends to just above the nest, a final strategic manoeuvre in its arduous journey. With a calculated release, the Gulltide drops the Canpagurus directly in front of the nest. The impact shatters the crab's tough shell, breaking it open in a way that allows the gull's mate to access the succulent white meat inside without having to leave the safety of the nest. Exhausted but relieved, our Gulltide circles above, watching as its mate prepares to feast. The mission accomplished, its struggle through the cold, harsh conditions ends with the satisfaction of having secured a vital meal for the family. In the stark, icy expanse of the salt marsh, the Gulltides' sacrifice reaches its poignant culmination. The Canpagurus, now stripped of its tough shell, provides the female with a nourishing bounty of 180 calories—a crucial energy boost in these harsh conditions. As the female gulps down the sustenance, replenishing her strength and fortifying the eggs nestled in the safety of the nest, the male remains resolute.

Despite his exhaustion and wounds, our Gulltide refrains from feeding, prioritising the needs of his mate and their future offspring. The female, recognizing his sacrifice, tries to offer him some of the crab's remains, but he gently pushes it back with a weary wing, his eyes resolute. With one last, determined flap, he takes to the sky once more. This is a glimpse of the self-sacrificing nature of all male Gulltides in times of great distress, embodying the profound devotion and resilience inherent in their struggle for survival and family.

As the fifth day dawns, a subtle transformation begins to unfold. By midday, the relentless cold snap that has gripped the salt marsh for days starts to relent. The harsh, icy winds ease their relentless assault, and the temperatures gradually begin to rise. Our Gulltide, though still recovering from his arduous efforts, finds a renewed vigour as the warming air invigorates his tired wings. He has, over the past few days, successfully foraged enough to sustain both himself and his mate, delivering an additional 180 calories to bolster their strength. With the cold's stranglehold easing, the nest feels the first hints of relief. The oppressive chill that once dominated the landscape begins to lift, bringing a welcome respite to the beleaguered gulls.

Chapter Twenty-Two: Parental Potential Lv:2

As the midday sun casts a gentle warmth over the salt marsh, there is a palpable sense of enduring renewal as the second incubation week begins. We shall now turn our attention to the eggs, which have suffered the most during this cold ordeal.

Egg Size (cm)	Initial HP	Current HP	Temperature (°C)	Egg Status And Viability
Egg 1 (6cm)	50	30	< 34°C	Critical: 25% chance of failure
Egg 2 (6.5cm)	70	30	< 37°C	Struggling: 20% chance of failure
Egg 3 (7.1cm)	90	60	< 37°C	Viable: 15% chance of failure
Egg 4 (7.5cm)	90	80	37°C	Stable: 0% chance of failure

The future of these fragile eggs hangs precariously in the balance. The recent cold snap has started to ease, but its effects linger. The smallest egg, a mere 6.0 cm, has suffered greatly, its temperature dropping below the critical 34°C mark. With just 30 HP remaining, it now faces a grim 25% chance of failure. Another, slightly larger at 6.5 cm, teeters on the same precarious edge, weakened by the relentless chill.

Yet, there is a glimmer of hope. The larger eggs, particularly the 7.5 cm specimen, have managed to hold their ground, maintaining a steady temperature near the ideal 37°C. As the air begins to warm, the parents find new foraging opportunities, allowing them to devote more energy to protecting their young.

But in this delicate dance of life and survival, nothing is guaranteed. The days ahead are uncertain, and only time will tell if these tiny lives can overcome the odds or if nature has other plans in store.

As the biting cold of winter slowly recedes, the mating grounds stir with renewed energy, yet the effects of the harsh season still linger. The female Gulltide, though weakened and still recovering, becomes the stalwart guardian of her nest. With painstaking care, she tends to her clutch, her every movement a testament to the fierce dedication of motherhood.

Meanwhile, the male, equally drained from the cold snap, bravely embarks once more on the perilous quest for sustenance. His solitary journey, though marked by fatigue, is driven by an unwavering commitment to his family's survival. The dance between these devoted parents is a poignant reminder of nature's relentless cycle of life, as they navigate the fragile line between struggle and renewal. As the harsh grip of the cold snap loosens, the coastline begins its slow and graceful recovery. The icy winds ease, allowing the first gentle breaths of warmth to drift across the eastern shore. Once-frozen waters stir with life again, while salt marshes, silenced by frost, hum softly with insects and the rustle of thawed grasses.

Atop a sheltered hummock, where the Gulltide nest is nestled, the sun's rays begin to warm the earth, melting the last remnants of frost. The hummock, now softening under the sun, offers a protective perch from which the birds can survey the rejuvenating landscape. The air, once crisp and biting, carries a gentler breeze, as the coastline reclaims its vibrancy. Nature cautiously reawakens, reflecting the enduring resilience of life after winter's long, cold hold.

The cold snap had rendered foraging nearly impossible for the Gulltides. Their usual prey, like the Gastrosnail and Clamite, had burrowed deep into the frozen substrate, well out of reach. Ice had gripped the Eastern Coastline, turning once-bountiful rock pools and mudflats into barren, inaccessible traps. Even the Mackerlure, a crucial food source, had vanished into deeper waters, leaving the Gulltides to struggle against the elements with dwindling reserves. But now, as the cold and icy conditions thaw, a transformation unfolds. The salt marsh, no longer sealed by the cold's icy grip, offers new opportunities.

The warming environment beckons Animara back to the surface, and the mudflats teem with life once more. For the Gulltides, this signals the chance to explore a broader diet. The thaw brings with it a promise of renewal, a feast waiting to be discovered among the softening sands and emerging pools. The Gulltides' struggle against starvation gives way to cautious optimism as nature tilts back towards balance.

As the cold snap fades, the male Gulltide takes full advantage of the warming air currents, despite his weakened state. He forages over an eight-to-ten-mile radius, making multiple trips between two food caches. His determined efforts yield approximately 800 calories stored in each cache, helping restore vital reserves. Along the way, he consumes 200 calories from a large Mackerlure, bolstering his strength. Upon returning to the nest, he proudly presents a rare Gastrosnail, a water bug-type Animara packed with 230 calories, offering it to his mate for her nourishment. The sight of him sharing this bounty highlights the pair's enduring bond as they care for each other amidst the still fragile environment. Although the weather is improving, the Gulltides and their eggs are not out of danger, and their survival remains uncertain in the slowly recovering landscape.

As the warming coastline recovers from the cold snap, so too are our Gulltide parents. Researchers have observed that *Larus Aquatilis* (Gulltide) unlocks inherited genetic skills after the second week of incubation—skills that only emerge when their XP falls within a certain range and then vanish when the mating season ends only to return the following year. The female Gulltide has developed the Nurturing Shift, a crucial behaviour where she carefully rotates the eggs each day. Although she had been turning the eggs before this ability's activation, they didn't gain the HP or XP benefits until the skill was unlocked. Now, with each careful turn, the eggs recover 5 HP and gain an additional 5 XP, boosting their development. The male has unlocked his Sentinel Instinct, a crucial ability that sharpens his awareness and strengthens his defences while guarding the nest. This skill increases his perception radius by 15%, allowing him to detect threats earlier, and grants a 10% boost to his health, making him more resilient in protecting the nest.

Each successful defence against predators rewards him with up to 500 XP, encouraging his vigilant efforts to safeguard his future offspring. A side effect of this parental unlock is that 5% of this earned XP is automatically transferred to the eggs, enhancing their growth and development. This unique blend of protection and XP-sharing means that every defensive action he takes not only shields the nest but also directly contributes to the healthy hatching of the eggs, ensuring the survival of their young.

As the second week unfolds, the Gulltide pair, having nearly regained their full strength after the brutal cold snap, find their vitality and caloric intake steadily improving. The male, now fully restored, takes on the role of vigilant guardian with renewed determination, while the female soars gracefully through the sky, her foraging efforts crucial for their survival.

Unbeknownst to them, however, the bulk of their XP and resources have been unintentionally allocated to the larger eggs. This misdirection has severely impacted the smallest egg, causing its HP and XP to plummet by a dramatic 45%. Despite their tireless efforts, the condition of the smallest egg continues to worsen.

As evening approaches, the female returns to the nest, her heart weighed down with concern. Utilising her Nurturing Shift ability, she meticulously turns the eggs, pouring all her hope and care into the fragile life within the smallest egg. With each careful adjustment, she clings to the hope that her devoted attention might still offer a chance for survival.

Chapter Twenty-Three: Sentinel Disputes

In the fading light of late afternoon, the salt marsh on the outskirts of the mating grounds is quiet, a place seemingly frozen by the lingering grip of winter. The hummocks, small islands of reeds and grasses, rise above the water, offering shelter and protection to those lucky enough to claim them.

Our male Gulltide perches atop a gnarled piece of deadwood, its weathered branches rising from the shallow pools like twisted fingers. From this high vantage point, he watches over his nest on the nearest hummock, his mate resting beneath the reeds, her body curled around two fragile eggs.

He scans the horizon. The last vestiges of the cold snap have left the air sharp, and the marsh remains damp and still. His mate is tired; the bitter cold of recent days has sapped her energy, leaving her to spend most of her time conserving warmth for the eggs beneath her. The eggs, speckled and pale, their delicate forms require constant care. The cold has slowed their development, and any disturbance now could prove disastrous. His mate's health is fragile, her caloric intake just enough to keep her warm. In this delicate balance, it falls to the male to defend their nest and ensure their future.

Suddenly, a piercing call echoes through the marsh. The male's body tenses. A rival Gulltide sweeps low over the water, his eyes fixed on the nest below. Their prime nesting spot—a hummock safe from flooding and most predators—has drawn attention. The rival circles closer, his intent clear: he means to drive the defending male away and claim the nest for himself.

Our male ruffles his feathers and rises from his perch. His Sentinel Instinct, honed by the demands of the breeding season, activates, sharpening his senses and boosting his defensive capabilities. His awareness of his surroundings increases, and his body responds to the threat, his HP rising from 85% to 95%. With a loud, guttural cry, he spreads his wings wide in a display of dominance, warning the intruder to keep his distance.

But the rival Gulltide is undeterred. He knows that securing a prime nesting site now could give his mate a chance to lay her eggs in safety. He swoops low, aiming for the nest. Our male, however, is not one to back down. His instincts flare—this is his territory, and his eggs are under his protection. The two birds meet in a flurry of wings and beaks. The rival Gulltide strikes first with a fierce Wing Attack, hoping to knock the defending male from his post.

But our male's heightened awareness allows him to dodge the blow. He counters with a sharp Peck, his beak finding purchase on the rival's wing. A screech of pain echoes through the marsh, but the intruder recovers, circling back for another strike.

For the next hour, the two birds engage in a fierce aerial duel. Our male Gulltide's Sentinel Instinct keeps him sharp, anticipating his rival's movements with uncanny precision. Each time the rival dives toward the nest, the defending male counters, driving him back with precision strikes. The stakes are high—both birds know that losing this battle means risking the future of their offspring. Growing tired, the rival makes a desperate final attempt. He dives straight for the nest, his wings cutting through the cold air like knives.

But with one final surge of energy, the defending male rises high into the sky. With a powerful downward sweep of his wings, he unleashes his strongest attack—Air Cutter. The gust of wind slams into the rival Gulltide, knocking him backwards and sending him tumbling through the air. Defeated, the rival screeches one last time before retreating into the mist beyond the marsh.

As the victorious male Gulltide watches his rival disappear, his Sentinel Instinct fades, but not without reward. His defence has earned him an additional 500 XP, and, as he returns to his nest, 2% of his XP is transferred directly to their eggs, accelerating their growth and bringing them closer to hatching. His mate stirs as he approaches, her pale eyes meeting him in silent gratitude. She shifts slightly, ensuring the eggs remain warm and safe. The marsh returns to its peaceful state, the air heavy with the approaching twilight.

The male Gulltide, ever vigilant, resumes his watch, knowing that the threats are never far. But for now, his nest is safe, and his mate and eggs are secure. He settles beside her, ready to defend his territory again should the need arise. This aggressive territorial behaviour is not unique to our male Gulltide but is, in fact, a defining characteristic of the species. Gulltides, like many coastal birds, are fiercely protective of their nesting sites, particularly during the breeding season when competition is at its peak. The coastal salt marshes, with their elevated hummocks, offer prime nesting grounds — safe from flooding and predators — but such valuable real estate is scarce. This drives the species into intense rivalry, where males must defend their nests from intruders to secure a future for their mates and offspring.

This behaviour becomes even more pronounced after events like the recent cold snap. The harsh weather depletes resources, weakens birds, and delays breeding cycles. When conditions ease, there is a sudden rush for the best territories, as every pair strives to recover lost time.

The shift in weather forces Gulltides to act with heightened urgency, knowing that delayed incubation could jeopardise their chances of successful hatching. The male's protective instincts, including his Sentinel Instinct, become even more critical in these moments. Such behaviour, though aggressive, is deeply rooted in survival. Gulltides invest tremendous energy into raising their young, and any disruption to the nest, especially in times of environmental stress, could endanger their efforts to pass on their genes.

Chapter Twenty-Four: Elder Symbiosis

As the territorial dispute raged below, three elder female Gulltides hovered high above, their wings beating slowly against the dawn light. These aged caretakers, identifiable by their faded plumage, have a unique role in the marsh. No longer breeding themselves, they fly from nest to nest, offering younger pairs a chance to rest, forage, and gather strength.

Circling cautiously in the sky, they waited. They couldn't descend until the conflict was over and the threat to the nesting grounds had passed. Though their presence is vital, it must come at the right moment, when peace returns and their gentle, supportive role can be fulfilled.

After nearly an hour, the battle subsided. The rival Gulltide retreated, leaving the tagged male exhausted but victorious.

Seeing their opportunity, the elder Gulltides sweep down from the sky, their flight slow and purposeful. Each head toward a different nest, ready to offer the much-needed relief the younger pairs have been waiting for.

One elder approaches the nest of our tagged pair. Still on edge from the recent fight, the young male watches her carefully as she lands nearby. Her arrival is marked by a series of soft trills. She moves gently toward the nest, not to take control, but to offer companionship—a quiet, comforting presence. Wrapping her wings, not around the eggs or the parents, but around the nest itself, she signifies her intent: she has latched onto this nest, not as a protector in the strictest sense, but as a moral supporter. From this moment on, the elder Gulltide becomes part of the family. While she won't defend the eggs from predators or provide physical protection, her calming presence offers reassurance to the parents. With her there, they can take the time they need to forage, stretch their wings, and regain their strength, knowing their nest is never left alone. In return, the relationship becomes reciprocal.

By welcoming the elder into their family, the tagged pair assumes a new responsibility: they will now forage not only for themselves but for her as well. It is a mutual exchange, a bond that benefits both the elder and the young parents. As they take to the air seeking food, the male Gulltide sets out on a four-mile circular route around the two females below. With each lap covering roughly two miles, he completes this flight plan twice, circling back every fifteen minutes to check on them, keeping a vigilant eye on the elder and his mate.

Meanwhile, the other two elder Gulltides, having landed briefly at nearby nests, choose not to establish the same deep connection as the first elder has. Their visits are fleeting, providing only a temporary respite before they take flight again, gliding gracefully across the marsh. By morning, they will have moved on, continuing their journey from nest to nest as needed. While their role may be less consistent, it remains crucial; these brief encounters give the younger parents a moment of rest, a chance to catch their breath amid the demanding task of raising their broods. This transient support, though short-lived, offers encouragement and reassurance, reminding the young pairs that they are not alone in their endeavours.

As the elder Gulltides depart, the younger parents feel the weight of their responsibility settle back upon them, yet they carry with them the lingering warmth of connection, knowing that help, even if temporary, is just a flight away. This behaviour, while rare in the animal kingdom, comes naturally to the Gulltides. The elder females, having completed their journeys of raising offspring, turn their attention to nurturing the next generation. By choosing to assist specific nests, they forge a unique bond with the young parents, offering a steady presence that brings comfort and reassurance. These matriarchs become a vital part of the family unit, offering emotional and practical support.

Ensuring that the breeding pairs remain strong, healthy, and undistracted as they focus on raising their young. Their wisdom and experience serve as a guiding light, fostering an environment where the fledglings can thrive.

In this cooperative dynamic, the older females impart valuable knowledge, teaching foraging techniques and survival skills that will empower the chicks as they grow. This nurturing network enhances the chances of survival for all involved, creating a legacy of resilience and interconnectedness within the community. For our tagged male Gulltide, the elder's presence offers more than just a chance to rest; it brings a sense of calm to the nest, allowing him and his mate to leave their eggs with confidence. As the day wears on and the sun rises higher, the elder Gulltide remains by the nest, her wings folded calmly, her eyes scanning the horizon. She will build a small nest of her own nearby in the coming days, creating a permanent presence within the territory.

Her role is quiet but indispensable; her unwavering support ensures that this young pair has every chance to succeed. Through her care, she fosters an environment where growth can thrive. The future of this brood looks that much brighter, illuminated by her presence. With renewed purpose, the tagged male continues his foraging, completing his two-mile circuit again and again, each return reinforcing the shared bond that deepens with each passing day.

Meanwhile, the two females work diligently, weaving twigs and grasses to build a nurturing haven in the heart of the marsh. Their efforts intertwine, creating a sanctuary where life can flourish, vibrant and resilient against the challenges of the wild. Each moment spent together fortifies their connection, and the anticipation of new life fills the air with hope, promising a legacy that will echo through the marsh for years to come.

In the delicate tapestry of life, a remarkable synergy unfolds, fostering an environment ripe for growth. At the heart of this family unit, the elder Gulltide plays a pivotal role, enhancing the dynamics in profound ways. Her presence contributes a solid 10% increase to the male's experience points (XP) cap each day, boosting his foraging efficiency and resilience in the marsh. Simultaneously, she enriches the young female's "Nurturing Shift" ability, amplifying her parental skills by an impressive 10%.

Consider the symbiosis between certain plants and fungi, where the roots intertwine with mycelium to exchange vital nutrients, enabling both to flourish. Similarly, these young parents draw upon their shared experiences and support systems, cultivating an atmosphere that encourages their development. It is this powerful partnership that fortifies their resolve, allowing them to face the trials of parenthood with confidence and grace.

Just as nature meticulously crafts these bonds to ensure the survival of future generations, so too, do these families create a nurturing foundation. They weave together love, wisdom, and support, ensuring that the next generation will thrive in a world filled with both challenges and boundless possibilities. In this intricate dance of collaboration, the legacy of resilience and nurturing continues, illuminating the path for those who will follow.

Chapter Twenty-Five: A Spark of Relief

As dawn's first light begins to warm the coast. The salt marsh, once stark and frozen, now glistens with the soft shimmer of spring's return. Coastal grasses, resilient against the cold, sway gently in the revitalised breeze, creating a tapestry of vibrant green and gold.

Amidst this rebirth, the male Gulltide remains a vigilant guardian, his sharp eyes sweeping the horizon with unwavering focus. His plumage, now vibrant and shimmering in the morning light, contrasts sharply with the still-chilled marshland below.

The female Gulltide, embodying tireless dedication, tends to their precious clutch with gentle care. Her attention turns to the nest, which has suffered from the harsh conditions of the cold snap. With practised movements, she makes repairs, reinforcing the structure with fresh reeds and grasses. Each delicate adjustment ensures the nest remains a secure haven for their vulnerable eggs. The nest, an intricate assembly of coastal materials, is now lovingly restored, cradling the eggs in a snug, protective embrace.

The cold snap is now a distant memory, replaced by the harmonious symphony of the mating grounds. The air is alive with distant calls, the flutter of wings, and the soothing rustle of grasses reaching for the sun. Despite the surrounding bustle, the Gulltide parents remain undistracted. Their mission is far from complete, for the future of their brood, fragile and full of promise, rests beneath them. With a swift, graceful leap, the male Gulltide takes flight, his form slicing through the morning air, a silent beacon of hope and renewal.

As he ascends, the rising sun catches the iridescence of his feathers, casting a fleeting brilliance across the salt marsh. His flight is a testament to resilience, a promise of new beginnings, and a herald of the vibrant life that is soon to flourish. As we already know the status of the eggs, we shall now quickly check on the parents' stats.

Animara Metrics Table	
Name: Gulltide (Male) Scientific Name: Larus Aquatilis Height: 55cm (21.65 inches) Weight: 1,6625 grams (3.6 pounds) Wingspan: 1.5 metres (4.92 feet)	Name: Gulltide (Female) Scientific Name: Larus Aquatilis Height: 47 cm (18.5 inches) Weight: 1,500 grams (3.31 pounds) Wingspan: 1.3 metres (4.27 feet)

	Male	Female	Combined
HP Score	65%	90%	65%
Total Flight Time	38 Hours	42 Hours	80 Hours
Distance Travelled	120 Miles	150 Miles	270 Miles
Calories Consumed	1,000 Cal	2,350 Cal	3.350 Cal
XP Score	2,800 XP	7,584 XP	10,384 XP
XP Needed For Next Level	11,800 XP	7,150 XP	18.950 XP

System Notes
Male Gulltide The cold snap caused a 5% body fat loss and a 20% reduction in HP due to food shortages and harsh conditions. Energy drain also cut flight time by ten hours. Severe caloric deficit dropped by 50%, well below healthy levels. Reduced XP gain, missed targets
Female Gulltide The cold snap caused a 10% decrease in her HP, though the female was able to better manage the cold. Flight time was cut by five hours, with energy maintained. Caloric intake slightly increased to meet needs. Minimal XP loss occurred due to consistent activity.
Both Gulltides gaining boost from Elder Gulltide Caregiver 10% boosted aid given to each status effect in flux at present

As the male Gulltide soars high above, scanning the windswept marshes for food, the female remains steadfast on her nest, her sharp eyes flicking to the horizon. The stillness is broken not by alarm, but by a subtle, almost unnoticed communication. Just a few feet away, another female Gulltide tends to her own clutch of eggs. With a soft call—a gentle, familiar sound—they acknowledge one another. These low-level interactions, almost imperceptible to the untrained observer, create a delicate bond of reassurance between the mothers.

In this quiet moment, the colony's communal rhythm pulses gently in the background, a reminder that while they are isolated in their duties, they are not alone. The simple exchange calms them, providing comfort as they nurture the fragile lives beneath them. And so, life on the salt marsh continues, its beauty revealed in the smallest of gestures.

This quiet social communication is crucial during the nesting and incubation period. With the eggs so vulnerable, the ability to remain calm and focused is essential for their survival. The brief exchanges between the female Gulltides create a shared sense of vigilance, allowing each mother to maintain her concentration without the constant pressure of isolation.

By acknowledging each other's presence, they reduce stress, ensuring the eggs receive the necessary warmth and protection. In the delicate balance of life on the marsh, these low-level interactions are vital, helping the mothers guard their nests and giving the eggs their best chance to hatch.

As our male Gulltide glides along the coastline, he is joined by another—a familiar face. It's the male whose mate had been quietly communicating with our tagged female back at the nests. This moment of collaboration is rare. During the harsh cold snap, survival demanded single-minded focus. Each male, driven by instinct, dedicated himself entirely to his own mate and nest. Food was so scarce that working together went against every instinct; every scrap had to be fought for. But now, with the cold releasing its grip, the urgency shifts.

The need to feed not just themselves but their mates is pressing, and with it, a temporary truce is born. Together, they circle the waters below, scanning, searching. No longer competitors, but fleeting allies in the warming world, driven by a shared purpose. In this delicate dance of survival, even the fiercest territorial behaviours can be set aside—if only for a moment.

As the sun casts its golden hue across the coastline, the two male Gulltides glide with a mix of determination and reluctance, their wings slicing through the crisp air. This stretch, normally too far north for their nesting needs, presents an uncomfortable choice. Yet, the relentless push for food compels them to venture ten miles into the vibrant northern reaches of the reserve—a realm teeming with the energy of electric and fire-type fauna. The decision weighs heavily on their instincts, as they know the risks of unfamiliar territory.

Rather than vocalising, the gulls communicate through a graceful ballet of wing dips and rises—an elegant dance akin to pilots greeting each other in the vast sky. With each subtle movement, they signal intent and direction, forging a silent partnership in pursuit of survival.

Hours pass as they navigate these perilous waters, the sun tracing its path overhead. Suddenly, a silhouette emerges below, breaking the surface—a fleeting shadow that ignites their instincts. Reluctantly, but resolutely, they lock their gaze on the shape, knowing this moment may hold the key to nourishing not just themselves, but also the precious lives waiting back at their nests.

With renewed focus, the male Gulltides circle high above, their sharp eyes honing in on the silhouettes below—two shimmering Voltshadyn, each a bounty of 700 Calories, gracefully navigating the waters in search of their own mating grounds. These vibrant fish radiate electric hues that glimmer like beacons against the azure sea. As the gulls prepare to dive, the Voltshadyn sense their presence and instinctively unleash a barrage of electric attacks, launching volleys of Volt Surge that crackle through the air, sending ripples across the water's surface.

In perfect synchrony, the gulls dip and rise, expertly evading the initial onslaught with agile manoeuvres. They twist and turn, weaving through the aquatic chaos as electrifying bolts sizzle past them, narrowly missing their feathers. Each evasive action is a testament to their finely tuned instincts, honed through seasons of survival.

Yet, the Voltshadyn are relentless, launching successive Water Blast attacks that illuminate the sea in flashes of blue and gold. Amidst the flurry of electric sparks, the male Gulltides execute a daring manoeuvre, unleashing Aerial Fog, a clever status effect move that envelops the Voltshadyn in a shroud of mist. This momentary distraction slows their movements just enough.

Seizing the opportunity, the gulls plunge into the water, talons outstretched, piercing the fluid embrace of the sea. With precise strikes, they manage to snag the two glimmering Voltshadyn, each fish firmly grasped in their claws, their vibrant scales flashing defiantly in the sunlight.

As they emerge from the water, both gulls feel the lingering effects of the electric attack coursing through them. The paralysing strike has taken its toll: with a daunting ten miles to fly back to their nests, they know each mile will be a challenge. For every two miles they fly, they lose 100 XP and 25% of their HP. Every flap of their wings feels heavier, the journey back fraught with risk and uncertainty.

With great determination, they begin their ascent, hearts racing with the thrill of victory, knowing their hard-won bounty will nourish not just themselves but also their waiting mates and the elder. The coastline stretches below as they soar into the uncertain sky, united in their shared struggle and unwavering commitment to the future.

Chapter Twenty-Six: Citrabella

At last, the male Gulltides return to the familiar expanse of their nesting grounds, their wings heavy with exhaustion and the weight of their hard-won prize. With a final effort, our tagged Gulltide reaches his nest, presenting the shimmering Voltshadyn to his waiting mate. This rare catch, fought for against the odds, represents not only survival but the enduring bond they share. Eagerly, they tear into the fish, each consuming half, replenishing their energy with the 350 vital calories needed after the arduous journey.

But the toll of the battle is clear. His mate, ever vigilant, notices the tremor in his wings and the stiffness in his limbs, the unmistakable signs of the paralysing shock from Voltshadyn's attack. She approaches with tender care, gently preening him, smoothing his ruffled feathers with precise strokes of her beak. This intimate act is more than a gesture of grooming—it is a quiet expression of love and solidarity. Her soft touches remove debris, but more importantly, they provide comfort and reassurance in the wake of his ordeal.

Despite her efforts, the effects of the electric strike linger. His wings and limbs remain gripped by an electrified paralysis, a condition that could last days, exacerbated by the elemental advantage of the Voltshadyn. For the time being, all he can do is remain in the nest, his body rendered immobile by the lingering shockwaves coursing through him.

The female, sensing his helplessness, takes to the skies once more, resuming her foraging duties. The male is left to recover with the Elder Gulltide, guarding their precious eggs as best they can, his condition a reminder of the unforgiving challenges of the salt marsh. For now, survival depends on his mate, while he remains nest-bound, waiting for the paralysis to fade. The female Gulltide remains close to the nest, never venturing more than a two-mile radius. Her mission is clear: to gather seeds, nuts, and fruits that will sustain her. Yet instinctively, she knows there are certain seeds and fruits capable of mending status effects, like the paralysing shock her mate now suffers. Her search is urgent and purposeful.

The female Gulltide glides over the salt marsh, her keen eyes ever watchful as they sweep across the landscape below. She navigates the delicate boundary where marshland meets the uplands, searching for the elusive Citrabella *(Citrabella fructus)*.

This resilient plant, typically found in the coastal dunes, sometimes ventures into these saltier regions, offering its vivid yellow-orange berries to those sharp-eyed enough to spot them. For the Gulltide, the Citrabella berries are more than just nourishment, each berry offering around 25 Calories each—they are also a tonic, packed with nutrients that can relieve status conditions.

Her flight is deliberate, a graceful loop as she circles the skies, her path tracing a figure of eight across the marsh. She dips low, skimming the grasses, then rises, scanning the horizon with unbroken focus. In the span of an hour, she has travelled nearly four miles, yet the bright berries she seeks remain hidden from view. Still, she does not falter. The Gulltide is a creature of patience, well-versed in the rhythm of this landscape, where persistence is as essential as the wind beneath her wings. For now, the Citrabella eludes her—but in the wild, nothing stays hidden forever. The search will go on.

Having found the Citrabella, and clutching it tightly in her grasp, the female Gulltide turns to make her way back to the nest. The triumphant moment is shattered as she catches the urgent warning calls of a neighbouring mother, a frantic cacophony that sends a chill through her veins. Danger lurks near the nests, and instinct overrides hunger. She drops her precious prize, channelling every ounce of her energy. With fierce determination, she converts nearly 50% of her overall experience into raw power, propelling herself to dart through the air with breathtaking speed. As the nest comes into view, the threat crystallises into a chilling reality—a Toxipurr, once frozen in the grip of the Nautilix, is back and fixated solely on the tagged Gulltides' nest. Its eyes gleam with malevolent hunger, dismissing all other potential meals. Once a Toxipurr catches the scent of its prey, it locks onto the trail with an intensity that borders on obsession, stalking its every move.

The predatory feline Animara will follow its quarry relentlessly, tracking, stalking, and ultimately hunting until it secures its prize. The air thickens with tension as the Gulltide accelerates, her heart racing against the impending doom. With each beat of her wings, she knows that the survival of her offspring hangs in the balance, and she must act swiftly to thwart this merciless hunter. The stakes have never been higher. As the female Gulltide soars through the air, her stat tag rapidly registers another 20% XP drop, translating into a surge of energy that fuels her frantic flight. Below, the menacing Toxipurr closes in on their nest, its predatory gaze locked onto the paralyzed male, who struggles to fend off the attacker with feeble water-based strikes. But in his weakened state, each splash only serves to irritate the relentless hunter. Time is running out; in mere minutes, the Toxipurr will secure its meal, and there's nothing the male can do to protect their offspring.

This dire situation triggers a further 20% reduction in the female's energy, igniting a burst of "hysterical strength." This spontaneous reaction, born from extreme distress in the face of imminent danger, can unleash remarkable power. Just as a human mother may lift a car to save her child, the Gulltide now channels every ounce of her instinctual might, racing against fate to save her family.

In a tense and unforgiving landscape, the female Gulltide swoops with precision, her sharp eyes locking onto the predator below. Recognition flickers—a moment of dread. The Toxipurr, sleek and menacing, is the same creature that stalked her weeks ago, relentless in its pursuit, intent on making her its meal. Now it prowls closer to her nest, undeterred by her presence. Her mate, still paralyzed from the Voltshadyn's attack, makes a valiant effort, launching weak, watery attacks that barely reach the ground. His strength is nearly spent, and his attempts do little more than irritate the Toxipurr. Poison pulses through its sleek form as it moves with lethal precision. This is no ordinary predator, and the Gulltide knows it. Already weakened, she is running on barely 35% of her health. With what little energy she has left, she dives through the air, summoning all her remaining strength to unleash a desperate Gale Surge.

The gust strikes hard, scattering dust and debris, but the Toxipurr merely flinches. The blow is little more than a distraction, and the predator's health, still at a formidable 85%, is barely affected. Ignoring its airborne opponent entirely, the Toxipurr locks onto the nest, driven by an unwavering instinct. Without hesitation, it fires a string of Venom Lash attacks, each venomous projectile hitting with pinpoint accuracy. The impact is devastating.

The nest, her paralyzed mate, and their fragile eggs are sent tumbling across the hummock floor. The Gulltide cries out in desperation, her strength slipping away as she watches the predator close in, her body weak, her health now dangerously low. Time is running out, and with it, the survival of her family.

The venomous strike of the Venom Lash has wrought devastation far beyond mere destruction; it has shattered the very heart of the Gulltide's nest. The largest and most viable egg lies in ruin, its delicate shell broken, the once-promising chick inside now lifeless. This loss ignites a fierce blaze of anger within the female Gulltide. It's a primal fury that courses through her veins, awakening something extraordinary. As her emotions swell, she feels a surge of power, propelling her beyond her level 6 status and straight to level 10.

In a breathtaking transformation, feathers shimmer with iridescence, glowing with vibrant hues of blue and green. The air around her crackles with energy and, as if the very essence of the salt marsh responds to her grief and rage, she evolves into a magnificent Waveplume. Her wings grow larger and more powerful, and her beak sharpens, ready to unleash her newfound abilities. But the moment is not hers alone. As the bright light envelops her, it extends to her mate, reigniting the bond they share. He, too, begins to change, his form illuminated in radiant energy. With his evolution, the status effect of paralysis is finally lifted, restoring his strength.

Together, they evolve into regal Waveplumes, side by side, rising as a formidable duo. Forged from loss yet brimming with newfound

Chapter Twenty-Seven: Tidal Waves of Pain

The salt marsh lies unnervingly still, the air thick with the tension of a moment suspended in time. The sacred ground of the Avian Animara, once a refuge of peace and whispered wind, is now poised on the edge of violence. The newly evolved Waveplumes stand before their nest, wings quivering, feathers bristling with anticipation. The sky above is bruised with the last light of day, casting a haunting glow over the marsh. Across the reeds, the Toxipurr prowls, its emerald eyes gleaming with predatory malice.

For what feels like an eternity, neither side moves, locked in a tense standoff. The Toxipurr, sleek and venomous, is a picture of lethal grace. It watches the Waveplumes, muscles coiled like a spring, waiting for the perfect moment to strike. Its claws dig into the mud, droplets of poison dripping from its fur, turning the very earth beneath it toxic. The air hums with dark energy as the predator sizes up its prey.

Then, without warning, the silence shatters.

The Toxipurr lunges forward, claws flashing in the dim light, eyes blazing with venomous intent. The Waveplumes react in a burst of motion, their wings snapping open with a whip-crack of feathers. The marsh explodes into chaos.

The male Waveplume rises first, surging into the air with a defiant screech, trailing a misty wave of water that hovers around his form. With a flick of his wings, he summons a deluge of marsh water from the reeds, launching it in a spiralling torrent toward the Toxipurr.

But the predator is quick. It twists in midair, narrowly avoiding the blast of water, landing with a splash in the shallows. It snarls, its tail lashing violently as it retaliates, flinging a cloud of poisonous mist toward the Waveplumes. The female, still grounded near the nest, spreads her wings wide, summoning a swirling current of wind that collides with the toxic cloud, dispersing it into harmless vapour.

Her eyes flash with determination—this is her home, and she will not let it fall. Undeterred, the Toxipurr strikes again, this time charging with lethal speed. Its claws swipe toward the male in the sky, but the Waveplume dives low, skimming just above the marsh's surface, wings carving through the air like blades. He circles the predator, drawing its attention as the female Waveplume, still on the ground, readies herself. Her body crackles with energy, water swirling at her feet, as she focuses her power into a single point.

With a shrill cry, she releases her attack—a concentrated blast of water that strikes the Toxipurr square in the chest. The force of the blow sends the predator staggering backward, mud and water splashing around it. Snarling in frustration, the Toxipurr digs its claws into the earth, trying to regain its footing. But the Waveplumes press their advantage. The male dives from above, wings shimmering with a silver glow as he strikes with razor-like precision.

The Toxipurr swipes back, but its movements are slower now, weakened by the Waveplumes' relentless assault. Its once-glowing eyes now flicker with exhaustion, its breath coming in ragged gasps. The predator knows it's losing, but its pride refuses to surrender.

With a final desperate roar, the Toxipurr leaps high, summoning the last of its toxic energy. Poisonous mist swirls around it, but the Waveplumes are ready. Together, they summon a gust of wind and water, their attacks combining into a powerful vortex that engulfs the predator.

The poison dissipates in the storm, leaving the Toxipurr exposed and vulnerable. The force of the combined attack sends the Toxipurr crashing to the ground. It lands in a heap, its sleek form battered, mud-caked, and breathless. It struggles to rise, shaking with effort, but it's clear the battle is over. The Waveplumes, still hovering in the air, watch as their foe falters. With a low, guttural growl, the Toxipurr lifts its head, its venomous eyes flicking one last glance toward the Waveplumes. It knows it has been defeated, but even in retreat, it refuses to show weakness. Slowly, it arches its back, claws scraping the earth as it forces itself upright.

With a final flick of its tail, the predator turns and bounds into the reeds, its sleek body disappearing into the shadows. The marsh exhales, the stillness returning like a sigh of relief. The Waveplumes land near their nest, their wings folding as they catch their breath. Victory is theirs, but they know the Toxipurr's retreat is not one of submission. It will wait, lurking in the depths of the marsh, ready for another chance. Yet, for now, the sacred ground belongs to the Waveplumes, their now-smaller family safe — for today.

As the sky darkens and the marsh returns to its ancient calm, the elder Gulltide, a grandmotherly figure to the young, hovers protectively over the broken shell of their most viable egg. The delicate remnants lie scattered in the soft mud, a potential life extinguished too soon. With a heavy heart, she gathers her feathers, weaving them into a shroud to envelop the shattered remains. Each plume is a testament to her love, an act of tenderness for the life that was never meant to be.

This behaviour, first observed by Animara researchers, has fascinated them for years. They documented how elder Gulltides engaged in elaborate rituals of mourning, demonstrating a profound emotional depth often attributed to human grief. These scientists marvelled at how the elder Gulltide's gentle care and sorrowful songs seemed to communicate a sense of loss not just to herself, but also to the grieving parents of the lost chick.

With a sorrowful determination, the elder positions herself beside the broken egg, offering her silent support, while the young parents grapple with the shock of their loss. Her presence is a balm for their hearts, reminding them that they are not alone in their grief. Regardless of the weather — be it biting winds or drenching rain — she remains steadfast, a pillar of strength in the face of despair, embodying the spirit of the marsh's elders.

As twilight deepens, the elder Gulltide tilts her head back and begins to sing, her voice a haunting melody that rises into the cool night air. The song flows like a gentle breeze, filled with warmth and sorrow, a lullaby for the lost chick that will never take its first breath.

Each note is a prayer, reaching out to the skies, inviting the spirits of the marsh to bear witness to her mourning. This act of song, observed by researchers, is a poignant reminder of the depth of avian emotional expression. The grieving parents, still reeling from their loss, draw closer to the elder, finding solace in her melody. One by one, other parental pairs arrive, their own hearts heavy with shared sorrow. In a rare and touching display, they gather around the elder and the broken egg, creating a circle of solidarity and support. Together, they join in the mourning, their voices harmonising with the elder's song as they bid the lost chick a final farewell.

In this act of devotion, the elder Gulltide not only grieves but also weaves a story of love, loss, and the enduring bonds of family. She embodies the cycle of life, where joy and sorrow dance together, each necessary for the other to exist. As night falls, her song continues to reverberate through the stillness, a reminder that even in loss, love endures, lingering like the stars that begin to twinkle overhead.

Though the Waveplumes remain vigilant against the shadows of the marsh, they are aware of the deeper currents of life that flow around them. The balance of nature is never final, and though predators may lurk, it is the bonds of family and community that ultimately define the heart of the marsh.

The elder Gulltide's vigil serves as a reminder that, even in the face of sorrow, the love shared within their community will always shine brightly, illuminating the path forward—a sentiment echoed by the researchers who have devoted their lives to understanding the mysteries of these remarkable creatures.

Chapter Twenty-Eight: Mourning Marsh

In the shadowed corners of the salt marsh, a yet more sombre scene unfolds. Our tagged newly evolved Waveplumes, a pair bound by both instinct and love, are joined by other nearby Gulltide pairs. Around twenty couples have gathered, not for the usual purpose of foraging or nesting, but to mourn the death of a chick.

While rare among gulls, such gatherings echo the behaviours seen in other bird Animara, like Corvaxum and Nocturnisa, which often assemble around a fallen member, cawing mournfully in what seems to be a communal funeral. These behaviours, in part, allow the group to learn of potential dangers but also reveal a profound sense of shared loss. The air over the marsh is thick with grief.

The newly evolved Waveplumes, still reeling from the loss of their young, stand silently at their shattered nest. But they are not alone.

The Alpha Waveplumes, the towering guardians of the colony, descend from their perches, their imposing forms softened in mourning. With wings held low and heads bowed, they stand beside the grieving couple, their usual fierce presence transformed into a quiet reverence.

Around the tagged Waveplumes, their plumage dimmed by sorrow, the community gathers in sombre unity. Where their raucous cries once filled the sky, now only soft, reflective calls drift over the marsh, like a melancholic breeze moving through the reeds. The colony stands in silence, sharing in the weight of the loss.

As the gathering lingers, the Waveplumes begin to pay tribute in a gesture both solemn and touching. One by one, they gently place grass and small reeds around the lifeless chick—a behaviour rarely seen outside of Walrune rituals. These seemingly ancient rock and water-type Animara are known for laying objects near their dead as a form of acknowledgement and respect. This simple act speaks volumes about the bond these creatures share.

The marsh, often a place of survival and struggle, becomes a place of shared grief, the quiet calls of the Waveplumes drifting across the winds. This rare act of mourning is a deeply emotional display, offering a glimpse into the inner lives of these often-overlooked birds. In a scene both haunting and beautiful, the gulls gather in silence, their usually animated calls hushed to a near-whisper. They stand shoulder to shoulder, forming tight clusters around the fallen, their heads bowed low.

Each bird seems to recognize the weight of this moment, an instinctive understanding that transcends their daily survival routines. For a brief period, the relentless drive of life in the marsh pauses, replaced by an overwhelming sense of loss that permeates the air. The colony, bound together by more than just instinct, shares this grief collectively, their bodies stiff with sorrow. It is a powerful, almost sacred ritual, revealing the depth of emotion and social bonds within their community.

As the moment fades, life will resume, but the echoes of this collective mourning will linger in the marsh, a testament to their unspoken connections. Despite the tragic loss of their most viable egg, the freshly evolved tagged Waveplumes still face their future with renewed hope. With three remaining eggs nestled safely in their care, they seem determined to persevere. Their recent evolution has imbued them with greater strength and agility—abilities that will prove invaluable in the coming days.

According to the stat tag affixed to their wings, their capacity to forage and defend their young has nearly doubled. What once required long, arduous flights to secure food is now a more efficient endeavour. Their protective instincts, sharpened by this transformation, will ensure the safety of the precious eggs that remain. However, to properly care for these three, the Waveplumes will need to construct a larger, sturdier nest—one that can shelter and nurture their future brood. As the funeral gathering begins to disperse, the sombre mood slowly lifts.

One by one, the birds glide effortlessly into the air, their wings catching the soft currents as they peel away from the group. With grace and quiet purpose, they return to their nests, where life continues to await them. Though the loss still lingers, there is a subtle but unmistakable shift—a sense of resilience bolstered by their newfound strength. For these Waveplumes, evolution has not just altered their forms but reignited their resolve to protect what remains.

Once the grieving Gulltide pairings have taken their leave, only one remains—the revered Alpha pair, custodians of the colony's traditions and strength. In a profound gesture of solidarity, the Alphas approach our tagged Waveplumes, recognizing their kinship from an evolutionary standpoint. In the world of Waveplume and Gulltide flocks, evolution often signifies a deeper connection than mere genetics; it represents shared experiences, and the bonds forged through survival.

The Alphas lend their support, helping to transport the remaining eggs back to the base of the majestic Pinnacle Perch. This location, a thriving heart of the mating grounds, offers a bounty of forageable foods and a sanctuary amidst the bustling flock, far safer than the exposed edges of the salt marsh. This will also not be the first time our tagged Waveplumes will interact with the Alphas.

Together, they navigate the intricacies of their shared world, each wingbeat resonating with the understanding that survival is a collective endeavour. Here, nestled among the heart of their mating ground community, the tagged Waveplumes find not just a place to build their nest but a renewed sense of belonging in the vibrant tapestry of life that envelops them.

As our tagged female Waveplume nestles the eggs securely beneath her wings, the other three evolved avian Animara set off to gather materials for the nest at the base of the Pinnacle Perch. Unlike the precarious salt marsh where their previous nest lay vulnerable to harsh winds and tides, this new location offers a stable, elevated foundation.

Formed from a series of flat, weathered boulders, the perch rises just a few metres above the surrounding terrain, commanding yet blending seamlessly with the landscape. Our tagged male Waveplume flies over fifteen miles of coastline, his evolved eyes scanning the shorelines with remarkable precision. He selects only the finest materials—strong, resilient twigs from coastal shrubs, fibrous strands of dried seaweed washed ashore, and flexible reeds to weave a durable structure. An hour later, the Waveplumes reconvene at the base of the Pinnacle Perch, each returning with their carefully selected finds.

The nest-building begins with painstaking precision. The Waveplumes weave the reeds into the natural crevices of the boulders, creating a sturdy framework. They secure the structure with seaweed, allowing for flexibility against strong coastal winds, and line the nest with soft down, making it a warm and protective haven.

Finally, as the last touches are made, the tagged female Waveplume gently settles her three remaining eggs into their new home. With only a week left before hatching, the abundant resources and safety of the Pinnacle Perch will make all the difference in ensuring the survival of the brood.

Chapter Twenty-Nine: The Duke and Duchess

As the first light of last week's dawn spills across the salt marsh, our newly evolved Waveplumes rest at the foot of the Pinnacle Perch. This majestic formation of flat, weathered boulders rises just a few metres above the marsh, offering a commanding view of the salt marsh's rugged beauty.

Around the perch, tall reeds sway gently in the cool breeze, their whispers carried over the still waters that glisten in the morning light. A delicate mist clings to the landscape, as the marsh slowly awakens to the sounds of distant birds and rustling leaves.

Nestled together, the Waveplumes sleep, their bodies entwined in a protective embrace around their remaining eggs. Even in slumber, their warmth shields the fragile shells beneath them, ensuring they are kept safe from the early morning chill.

This dawn may mark the first light of the last week for incubation, but it is far from the end of their journey. Once the eggs hatch, a new chapter begins—a struggle for survival intertwined with the significance of the Pinnacle Perch itself.

With their newfound status within the flock, the tagged male and female Waveplumes each take on distinct yet complementary roles under the leadership of the Alpha Waveplumes.

The male Waveplume, swift and vigilant, assists the Alpha in patrolling the marsh's borders, scouting for potential threats and securing key foraging grounds. His agility allows him to cover vast areas quickly, ensuring the safety of the flock's resources.

Meanwhile, the female, nurturing and wise, works closely with the Alpha female, overseeing the care of eggs and younglings within the flock. Her role involves mentoring younger mothers and ensuring the delicate balance of warmth and protection within each nest.

Together, the pair supports the Alpha Waveplumes in maintaining harmony within the flock, mediating disputes, and ensuring that resources are shared fairly among all members.

Their combined efforts solidify their standing as trusted leaders, integral to the survival and unity of the flock. Their evolution has also shifted their standing within the flock.

No longer just another pair, they are now considered leaders. Though the Alpha Waveplumes still hold the seat of power atop the Perch, our newly evolved pair occupy a role akin to that of a Duke and Duchess.

With their nest at the base of the Perch, they've inherited both honour and responsibility, guiding others within the flock. Their presence at the foot of the Perch, where leadership is decided, signifies their rise in status, a testament to the evolving hierarchy within the Gulltide community.

During their mating pilgrimage to the Coastal mating grounds, our tagged avian Animara faced a relentless barrage of challenges. They braved biting cold snaps, lurking predators, and the heart-wrenching pangs of loss. Yet, through these trials, they have evolved into devoted and resilient parents.

Each hardship has strengthened their bonds and sharpened their instincts, transforming vulnerable fledglings into vigilant guardians. They have learned the rhythms of survival and the art of nurturing, weaving a delicate balance of care and vigilance essential for their offspring.

Now, let us pause to explore their new statistics reflecting their remarkable evolution.

Animara Metrics (FINAL EVOLUTION)	
Name: Waveplume (Male) Scientific Name: Pelecanus Oceanus Height: 160 cm (63 inches) Weight: 6,000 grams (13.23 pounds) Wingspan: 305 cm (120 inches)	Name: Waveplume (Female) Scientific Name: Pelecanus Oceanus Height: 150 cm (59 inches) Weight: 5,500 grams (12.13 pounds) Wingspan: 290 cm (114 inches)

	Male	Female	Combined
Current HP Score	106%	125%	106%
Total Flight Time	60 Hours	52.5 Hours	112.5 Hours
Distance Travelled	200 Miles	187.5 Miles	387.5 Miles
Calories Consumed	2,937.5 Cal	2,812.5 Cal	5,750 Cal
XP Score	5,062.5 XP	9,817.5 XP	14,880 XP
XP Needed for Next Level	13,687.5 XP	8,937.5 XP	22,625 XP

As the Gulltide family and newly evolved Waveplumes face the challenges of a rapidly shifting world, their evolutionary transformations bring a significant 25% boost—helping them cope with the taxing demands of their increased mass. Their new height, expanded wingspan, and greater weight put immense pressure on their bodies, requiring more energy, control, and endurance. This boost, triggered by their evolution, helps them manage the strain of their larger frames, ensuring they can still soar, forage, and protect their nests as nature demands. At this pivotal time, the presence of the elder Gulltide, a figure of ancient wisdom, becomes crucial. Her calming influence stabilises the nest, allowing the younger pair to recover from the physical toll of their evolution.

The elder's support provides a vital 10% experience boost, helping the pair adjust to their heightened limits. Meanwhile, the nurturing female continues to tend to the eggs, ensuring their warmth and safety, further aided by the elder's wisdom. Together, the 25% evolutionary boost and the elder's steady guidance form a critical balance.

With newfound strength and ancient care, the Gulltides and Waveplumes push through the burdens of their new mass, securing the survival of their family and future generations. As we enter the final week of incubation, the tagged Waveplumes's care is more crucial than ever. The eggs, now nearing hatching, rest under their vigilant watch so for one last time let's check out their unhatched stats.

Animara Metrics				
Egg Size (cm)	Initial HP	Current HP	Temperature (°C)	Egg Status and Viability
Egg 1 (6.0cm)	50 HP	62 HP	35°C	Improved: 5% chance of failure
Egg 2 (6.5cm)	70 HP	71 HP	37°C	Stable: 0% chance of failure
Egg 3 (7.1cm)	90 HP	86 HP	37°C	Stable: 0% chance of failure

The female Gulltide's recent evolution to a Waveplume, has enhanced her nurturing instincts. Her Nurturing Shift, once restoring 5 HP per day, now boasts a 25% increase, allowing her to heal 6.25 HP daily for each egg. This subtle yet significant improvement, combined with the elder Gulltide's ever-watchful aid, ensures the eggs receive the highest level of care.

The elder Gulltide, vigilant and protective, adds a further 10% boost to this ability, ensuring the eggs are kept warm and shielded from threats. As a result, Egg 1, once on the brink, has now recovered to 62 HP, cutting its failure risk to just 5%. Egg 2, with 71 HP, has fully stabilised, while Egg 3, already strong, now rests confidently at 86 HP with no chance of failure. The XP gained daily has also risen from 5-10 XP to 6.25-12.5 XP, accelerating their growth and development. Together, the evolved female's heightened instincts and the elder Gulltide's steadfast presence create a near-perfect system of protection and nourishment, giving the eggs an enhanced chance to thrive in this wild and untamed world. Nature, once again, shows us the intricate balance of survival.

With their brood now out of danger, our newly tagged Waveplumes navigate the bustling world around them, assured that their eggs are well cared for. They take to the skies alongside the Alpha Waveplume, wings stretching wide as they embrace the freedom of the open air. Below, both inexperienced and experienced parents alike tend to their eggs, all under the watchful eye of the elder Gulltide. This venerable guardian ensures that every nest is nurtured, fostering a sense of community and shared responsibility.

The anxious movements of the inexperienced parents, marked by a mix of eagerness and uncertainty, contrast with the calm confidence of their seasoned counterparts. As they flit between nests, offering beaks full of food and warmth, they all gain invaluable experience from the elder's gentle guidance. The sun casts a golden light across the rocky perch, illuminating this intricate web of care. Here, amid the sounds of nurturing calls, life continues its age-old dance, sustained by the bonds of kinship and the wisdom of generations.

Chapter Thirty: A Tender Moment

As the incubation period draws to a close, the coastal mating grounds pulse with a palpable tension, each moment infused with the promise of new life. The sea crashes gently against the rugged cliffs, its rhythmic ebb and flow a soothing symphony in this wild sanctuary. The air is rich with the briny scent of the ocean, invigorating all who call this place home.

Nestled among the rocky outcroppings of the Perch, our tagged female Waveplume sits resolutely on her cherished clutch of eggs. Her soft blue-grey feathers, fluffed against the cool coastal breeze, form a protective barrier against the elements.

Nearby, her devoted mate stands vigilant, his bright yellow eyes sweeping the horizon with unwavering focus. Each measured movement he makes reflects his activated Sentinel Instinct, a testament to his commitment to safeguarding their future brood. As the wind rustles through the grasses, he stretches his wings, embodying the very essence of vigilance.

This diligent mother has consistently performed her remarkable Nurturing Shift, expertly rotating the eggs each day to ensure even warmth and vitality. Through her unwavering dedication and meticulous care, every egg now stands at 100% health, fully viable and ready to embrace the world beyond the nest.

Above the cliffs, the calls of other Gulltides fill the air, harmonising with the commanding presence of the Alpha Waveplumes, who watch over this delicate dance of life. The mating grounds teem with activity, the scent of briny seaweed and damp earth wafting through the air, punctuated by the distant cries of predators patrolling the cliffs.

With incubation complete, the tagged parents, like their counterparts, have little left to do but wait. The hatching could take anywhere from one to three days, yet the atmosphere brims with anticipation.

Their synchronised movements—feeding, guarding, and nurturing—create a rhythmic pattern of life, echoing the ancient cycles of survival on this windswept coastline, where the promise of new beginnings hangs tantalisingly in the salty air.

With the anticipation of new life swirling in the air, our tagged Waveplumes glide gracefully on the wind currents, their long wings outstretched like sails catching the breeze. Effortlessly, they navigate the skies, whose mastery of flight allows them to traverse vast distances with ease.

As they soar over the shimmering blue expanse, a small skerry—a rocky islet surrounded by water—emerges on the horizon, beckoning them with its rugged charm and soft patches of vegetation. They descend gently, landing softly on the sun-kissed shores, where the rhythmic sound of the waves caresses the coastline, creating a tranquil symphony.

Once ashore, the Waveplumes engage in a tender moment, preening their feathers not merely to keep clean, but as a quiet expression of their love and devotion. Each gentle stroke becomes a metaphorical embrace, a way to reaffirm their bond in this serene setting. The skerry, with its vibrant flora and gentle breezes, offers a peaceful refuge. Here, surrounded by nature's beauty, they share whispered calls and soft nudges, relishing the intimacy of their connection.

After a time of tender connection on the skerry, our tagged Waveplumes once again take to the air, leaving the tranquil islet behind. With a powerful thrust of their wings, they ascend into the cerulean sky, the sun glinting off their soft blue-grey plumage. As they soar together, their bond deepens, each movement a graceful dance of unity. The vast ocean stretches below, teeming with life, and they begin to forage not just for their own sustenance but also for the Elder Gulltide, who waits at the nest. Together, they dive and swoop, their keen eyes scanning the shimmering waters for fish and crustaceans. As they glide gracefully over the water, they encounter a small school of the agile Animara known as Breezefin.

Renowned for their sleek bodies and shimmering scales, these delightful fish boast brilliant hues that echo the colours of the sky. More than just a visual feast, the Breezefin is a veritable treasure trove of sustenance. With a harmonious synchrony, our tagged parents engage in their delicate ballet of hunting, darting swiftly through the water to catch five of these calorie-rich morsels. Each Breezefin offers a generous bounty of approximately 220 calories, serving as a vital energy source for our sardine friends. As they feast, the sardines absorb not only the nutrients but also the essence of the sea, their bodies brimming with vitality as they prepare for the challenges that lie ahead.

As the tagged Waveplumes soar back toward their nest, perched on the rocky outcroppings of Pinnacle Perch, they engage in a remarkable display of aerial mastery. Gliding on the thermals, thanks to their expansive wings, which allow them to cover great distances with minimal effort. This two-mile journey not only serves as a return to their sanctuary but also as an opportunity to forage for sustenance, replenishing both their and the Elders' food caches. The male Waveplume, with keen eyes fixed on the horizon, scans the air for the tiniest movements. He expertly manoeuvres through the sky, tilting his wings and adjusting his body to harness the winds, much like an albatross navigating the open ocean. His sharp vision detects a variety of flying insect Animara, which flit about in the warm air. With each graceful swoop and agile dive, he captures these minuscule morsels, refuelling his energy reserves.

By the time Pinnacle Perch comes back into view, he has fully replenished his health and restored it to 100% vitality. But the need to forage continues. As the Waveplumes near their nest, an unspoken understanding passes between the pair, prompting them to divide their foraging efforts. With a sudden, deft U-turn, the male sweeps back out to sea, skillfully hugging the rugged coastline of their mating grounds. His expansive wings catch the wind as he rides the thermals, eyes keenly scanning the shimmering waters for the bounty that lies beneath.

Meanwhile, the female ascends higher, gliding above the dunes and coastal vegetation, her sharp eyes scanning for any signs of nourishment hidden among the vibrant flora. Almost in unison, they embark on a series of return trips to their caches, the male diving low to snatch up morsels while the female gathers insects and small crustaceans from the shoreline. Together, yet separately, they complete an impressive twenty-five, one-mile circuits in just two hours, at an average speed of twelve and a half miles per hour. This breathtaking ballet of efficiency showcases their remarkable endurance and synchrony as they tirelessly search for sustenance. By the end of the two-hour window, both their and the elder's caches are brimming with around 1,000 calories each.

As the sun begins its descent, casting a warm golden glow across the rugged coastline, the tagged Waveplumes pause briefly at their cache, their bodies glistening with vitality. Here, they discover a shallow rock pool, its surface shimmering with reflections of the sky above. Taking a moment to drink, they replenish their hydration, vital for their relentless foraging efforts.

At the pool's edge, they also find an assortment of nuts and fruits, a delightful bounty that offers approximately 100 calories. Each morsel invigorates them, providing the energy needed for the next leg of their journey. Once recharged, the pair makes their way back to the nest, where their delicate eggs await their tender care. As the elder Gulltide departs for her own nest to enjoy a well-deserved meal and rest, our tagged mother settles back into the nest, instinctively aware that it will not be long before the eggs begin to hatch.

This awareness is beautifully conveyed by a shimmering glow in her head plumage, a subtle signal to the male. With this shared understanding, the two tagged parents let out a series of happy, almost joyous Animara calls, filling the air with a melody that echoes through the flock, celebrating the promise of new life.

Chapter Thirty One: First Born

We are now a day into the hatching window, and the morning unfolds with the familiar routine. Our tagged male and female take to the air, working alongside the flock's Alpha couple. The male Gulltide aids in the defence of the mating grounds, a vital responsibility that requires vigilance as other creatures and rival flocks press the boundaries of this precious territory.

Meanwhile, the female turns her attention to the younger mothers embarking on their first mating season, offering encouragement and guidance. Together with the Alpha pair, they embody the balance of protection and nurture, their roles complementing each other in perfect harmony. As they patrol and assist, our tagged parents continue to learn, growing within the flock's social structure, while reinforcing the interdependence that governs this coastal landscape. Each day brings new insights into their place within the larger rhythm of Gulltide life.

The female Gulltide descends gracefully onto the salt marsh, her focus shifting from the skies to the nesting grounds below. Nearby, a group of younger mothers is huddled close, their first clutch of eggs nestled carefully within their hastily made nests. She is not alone. By her side stands the Alpha mother, a figure of wisdom and calm. Together, they move quietly among the inexperienced mothers, their presence reassuring. With a gentle call, the female Gulltide encourages one of the younger birds to adjust her nest, offering guidance on how to better shield her eggs from the cool coastal breeze. The Alpha mother joins in, her keen eyes surveying each nest, providing subtle corrections and advice. This mentoring is crucial; it ensures the next generation learns not only survival but how to thrive in this unpredictable environment. The young mothers watch closely, absorbing the lessons passed down from seasoned matriarchs who've endured these seasons before. Each interaction fosters a sense of community, and with every small adjustment, the nesting site becomes a little more secure.

Here, in the company of their elders, these young Gulltide mothers learn the vital balance of instinct and wisdom needed to raise the future of the flock. The female is about to head to another nest to offer aid when the call comes through, sharp and unmistakable. It rises from Pinnacle Perch, spreading like a ripple through the colony, but this is no ordinary call.

Only because of the almost regal standing the evolved Waveplumes hold within the flock does such a signal reach them. Normally, Gulltides would never abandon their nests, instead taking shifts to guard their eggs. Yet with the evolution of the Waveplumes, comes not just physical changes, but as previously discussed new duties within the flock's social order.

As protectors and mentors, they rely on the flock to help keep watch over their nests during these times. The colony responds in kind, a shared understanding that benefits all. With the call relayed, the female halts, and almost at once, the male leaves his patrol. Together, they abandon their duties and rush back, driven by instinct and responsibility and a parental bond.

The air is filled with quiet anticipation as the tagged parents fly back, and within minutes, they reach their nest nestled securely at the base of the towering Pinnacle Perch. The wise elder Gulltide gently hops aside, and the female Gulltide lowers herself into the nest, her warmth enveloping the three eggs. Outside, the male stands sentinel, watching both his mate and the horizon, ever alert.

Suddenly, a soft crack echoes through the rocks. The largest egg trembles, its surface fracturing into delicate lines. The parents turn their gaze toward the egg, united in purpose. With a final push, a tiny beak pierces the shell, slowly revealing a damp, downy head. The female watches closely, instinctively offering warmth and reassurance, while the male keeps a vigilant guard just beyond the nest, his eyes scanning for threats yet always returning to the hatching chick. Together, they witness the moment their efforts come to life, the new arrival safely emerging into the world.

The young chick, fresh from the confines of its egg, emerges into the world with a tentative struggle. Its tiny, wet body glistens in the soft light, trembling as it adjusts to its newfound freedom. Now that the first of the eggs has hatched, we are presented with a rare and wondrous opportunity to observe the new chick as it takes its very first breath of life. The delicate numbers—reflecting its health, stamina, and early strength—offer a captivating glimpse into the potential held within this fragile creature.

Animara Metrics Table	
Name: Gulltide (Newborn Chick- Male) Scientific Name: Larus Aquatilis Height: 7.1cm (2.79 inches) Weight: 350 grams (estimate) Wingspan: N/A (wings still developing)	
Current HP Score	90%
Total Flight Time	N/A Not flight-capable yet.
Calories Reserved	180 Calories
Calories Consumed	N/A Awaits first meal from parents
Current XP Score	150 XP
XP Needed For Next Level	N/A
System Notes	
<ul><li>XP frozen at Level 1 for the first 3 months.</li><li>Reserve is taken from stored calories from absorbed yolk at the moment of birth.</li><li>Maintaining ideal warmth at 35°C outside temperature 37°C</li></ul>	

Each statistic tells a story, shaped not only by the nurturing warmth of the nest but also by the devoted care of its mother, who watches nearby.

Unsteady limbs, still unused to movement, stretch out awkwardly, seeking balance in the warm nest below. The mother Gulltide, ever watchful, lowers her head with a gentle coo, nudging the chick softly with her beak. Each tender touch serves as a guide, encouraging the chick to take its first hesitant steps toward her. Its downy feathers, still damp, begin to fluff as it stumbles forward, emitting a faint, instinctive chirp.

The female Gulltide responds with a murmur, drawing her chick close. With delicate care, she tucks the fragile creature beneath her wing, offering the warmth and shelter it so desperately seeks. Safe in its mother's embrace, the chick grows still, settling into the soft cocoon of her feathers. Life, fragile and new, finds its footing under her protective care. Yet, like all younglings of the Animara, this chick finds itself in a unique phase during these formative days. Its XP and levels remain effectively frozen at Level 1, a status that will persist for the first three vital months of its existence. During this time, the chick will focus entirely on the essential tasks of survival—seeking nourishment and mastering the basic life skills necessary for its journey ahead.

Once this critical period has passed, the chick's XP and levels will begin to unfreeze, allowing it to access the accumulated XP it has stored while nestled in the safety of its egg. This stored experience will set its opening stats for the rest of its life, meaning that if it has gathered enough XP to reach Level 2 or even Level 3 while developing inside the egg, it will immediately hit that target once the unfreezing begins.

Gradually, its XP will continue to increase at a rate of 2% each week until it reaches the milestone of one year. At that point, its development will accelerate, allowing it to fully embrace its potential. In the gentle light of early dawn, the newborn Gulltide chick lies nestled within the warmth of its downy nest. Tiny, vulnerable, and just a few hours old, it is already the focus of an intricate, time-honed dance of survival. The chick, still absorbing the last remnants of its yolk sac, chirps softly, calling for the attention of its parents.

These avian guardians, majestic and ever-watchful, balance their responsibilities with delicate precision. One parent stands sentinel, shielding the fragile chick from the cold, while the other takes flight into the vast coastal skies, seeking sustenance from one of its caches. Their partnership is seamless—each return is met with a soft exchange. As nourishment is shared, the chick is carefully fed. This harmonious bond, built on trust and instinct, is vital for the Gulltide's survival in this delicate yet harsh world. Every action, every moment, is a testament to nature's enduring cycle of life.

The male Waveplume returns to the nest, gliding gracefully through the cool morning air. In his beak, he carries a small collection of wriggling insects, each rich with vital nutrients—around 15 calories apiece—critical for the survival of his newborn chick. As he lands softly beside the nest, the chick stirs, instinctively sensing its father's presence. The male tilts his head, peering down at the tiny, fragile creature, and offers a soft call, reassuring the chick that food has arrived.

With practised precision, the male gently taps his beak against the chick's, signalling it to open wide. The chick responds, beak agape, waiting eagerly. One by one, the insects are carefully deposited into the chick's throat. The male ensures each morsel is placed just right, allowing the newborn to swallow effortlessly. The chick gulps the food down, its energy slowly replenishing with each bite. The bond between father and offspring grows stronger with every delicate feeding, a vital act of care in these critical early moments of life.

Chapter Thirty Two: A Foraged Feast

As the soft glow of dawn spreads across the windswept shore, the female Waveplume sits serenely in her nest, her iridescent feathers catching the first light of day. Beneath her wings, her chick nestles close, its tiny body still fresh to the world, comforted by the gentle rise and fall of its mother's steady breath. Two unhatched eggs lie nearby, their smooth, pearl-like shells glistening with morning dew. Above, the sky is painted with the pale hues of early light, and the rhythmic sound of waves rolling ashore creates a soothing backdrop to this scene of new life.

High above, her mate soars gracefully through the coastal air, his strong wings slicing through the cool breeze as he scans the shimmering sea for food. Each dive he makes is a testament to their shared commitment, a perfect harmony of foraging and protection. Down below, the female watches over the fragile life in her care, her vigilant eyes reflecting the joy of the moment, knowing her chick and the remaining eggs are safe under her warmth.

As the male Waveplume soars above the shoreline, the once-crowded nesting grounds stretch out below him, now noticeably quieter. The flurry of activity that once filled the air as hundreds of Gulltides tended to their chicks has dissipated, with many taking to the skies and leaving behind their nests. In their absence, the coastline begins to breathe again, its resources—small fish, crabs, and other sea life—slowly returning to abundance.

But the now-empty nests won't remain vacant for long. From the Salt Marsh, familiar breeding pairs begin to arrive, not new faces, but those who had long nested elsewhere. These pairs are not starting fresh but simply relocating, much like humans moving homes. They bring with them their unhatched eggs or newborn chicks, carefully cradled as they settle into the recently vacated nests. These are also the same pairs that once stood in solemn support with our tagged Waveplumes when they mourned the loss of their chick.

These families will settle into the nests left behind, finding comfort in the same resources and shelter the shoreline provides, ensuring their young thrive in this now less crowded and bountiful place. In this familiar cycle, life carries on.

Around two miles off the shoreline, near the vibrant mating grounds, the tagged Waveplume male soars with unwavering purpose. His evolved eyes, now exquisitely attuned to detect larger prey, scan the waters for the elusive Venomari—a squid-like Animara, notorious for its toxic defences. Riding the coastal breeze, the Waveplume glides effortlessly, his wings carving arcs through the air as he senses the subtle shifts in the ocean currents below. Suddenly, his sharp gaze locks onto a faint ripple—an unmistakable sign of movement lurking beneath the surface.

His instincts have driven him to seek greater foraging finds. No longer does he settle for smaller fish; the Waveplume positions himself for a more complex and perilous hunt. Hovering with tension in his wings, he adjusts his angle for the perfect dive. In a swift, calculated motion, he plunges downward, transforming his body into a streamlined torpedo. As he breaks through the water's surface, a specialised protective membrane envelops his eyes, granting him a crystal-clear view of his surroundings.

Below him, the shimmering Venomari glows with an enchanting bioluminescence, its radiant light betraying its frantic attempts to evade capture. In this dance of predator and prey, the stakes are high, and the chase has begun.

With swift, powerful strokes of his webbed feet and the precise movements of his long beak, the Waveplume outmanoeuvred the squid in a breathtaking display of skill and determination. Triumphantly, he rises from the depths, clutching his catch, which offers an impressive 500 calories. Recognizing the critical importance of this bounty, he deposits it in a carefully hidden water-based cache, ensuring that his family can access this vital energy source when needed.

But the hunt is far from over; with the sun high in the sky, our intrepid Waveplume returns to the promising foraging ground several times throughout the day. On his second trip, he is met with success once more, capturing another Venomari, adding another 500 calories to his cache. Not content to rest, he ventures back yet again, where fortune smiles upon him once more. A final, skillful plunge yields a third Venomari, bringing his total haul to an impressive 1,500 calories. In this tireless pursuit of nourishment, each catch is not just a personal triumph but a crucial contribution to the well-being of his family, ensuring they have the sustenance needed to thrive in the ever-changing ocean world.

As the sun dips below the horizon, casting golden hues across the vast ocean, our tagged Waveplume returns from his foraging expedition, his wings outstretched in a graceful descent. Gliding down to the nest, he finds his devoted partner waiting patiently. Before departing, she uses her unique Nurturing Shift ability, gently transferring warmth and energy to the unhatched eggs—a vital act that fosters their development. In a smooth, practised exchange of duties, they swap roles, allowing her to join the Alpha Waveplume in assisting the inexperienced Gulltides of the flock, guiding them as they tend to their delicate unborn eggs and vulnerable day-old chicks.

The Alpha's steady leadership is crucial in helping these young mothers, including our newly tagged Waveplume, navigate the challenges of early parenthood and learn the ropes of becoming an Alpha female within the flock.

Now, the male Waveplume settles into the nest, assuming the role of caretaker with quiet determination. His watchful gaze falls on the fragile chick nestled beside him, while he vigilantly guards the remaining eggs. With unwavering devotion, he creates a sanctuary of safety, where life can flourish under his protection.

In this intricate balance of responsibilities, the bond between partners grows ever stronger, reflecting the remarkable resilience and cooperation necessary for survival in this ever-changing, dynamic world.

Here, family is everything, and together, they secure the future of their lineage. A few quiet hours pass as the male Waveplume dutifully tends to his chick, his focus unwavering. The air is still, save for the gentle rustling of his feathers as the coastal breeze flows across the nest. The rhythmic crashing of waves below seems to lull the world into a serene stillness. Yet, beneath him, a quiet transformation is taking place—one he does not notice.

One of the unhatched eggs, warmed earlier by his partner's nurturing shift, begins to stir. A faint crack appears on the fragile shell, almost invisible in the dimming light of dusk. Oblivious to this subtle event, the male carefully preens the tiny chick beside him, running his beak gently through its soft down, removing bits of debris that have gathered. The chick, still too young to fend for itself, snuggles closely beneath his protective wings as he occasionally offers it small bits of regurgitated food. His attention is fixed entirely on this young one, keeping it warm, fed, and safe from the cool evening air.

As the light fades and the ocean breeze cools, our tagged Waveplume father, ever vigilant over his growing chick, lets out a soft, gentle call. This time, his request is for the elder Gulltide, the wise matriarch of the flock. It's as if he's politely asking, "Can you please get us some food?"

The elder, attuned to the needs of the flock, rises from her nest and takes to the sky, her broad wings cutting gracefully through the air. She flies toward the water-side cache, where the day's bounty lies hidden beneath the surface, including the remains of the Venomari squid, now dead but preserved for later use. Moments later, she returns, clutching a torn piece of the Venomari's lifeless body, its bioluminescent skin still faintly glowing in the dim light. This small piece, though just a fragment, offers around 80 calories—enough to nourish the father and keep the chick sustained beneath his warm, protective wings. The elder, after delivering the food, will likely return to the cache for her own share, taking a similar portion to keep herself strong. In this intricate dance of survival, the water-side cache serves as a lifeline, ensuring the family's survival.

Chapter Thirty-Three: Strife and Pearls

As the hours drift by, the melodic calls of our tagged mother Waveplume echo softly on the breeze, carrying her presence back to the nest and telling them she will be back soon. Yet, within the cosy sanctuary, a quiet transformation unfolds. The faint sound of cracks reverberates as the smallest egg shows signs of life, each delicate fracture a herald of new beginnings. Oblivious to this miracle, the father diligently attends to the needs of his chick, feeding it small morsels from the chunk of Venomari provided by the elder.

With a careful, gentle motion, he tilts his head, expertly breaking off tiny pieces of the soft, nourishing flesh. He offers these morsels to the eager chick, who instinctively opens its beak wide, consuming about 20% of the 80 calories available. As the chick devours the nourishing food, the father savours the remaining portion, ensuring he, too, is replenished. In this moment of nurturing, he remains completely unaware of the precious life stirring within the egg nearby.

Finally finished with her vital duties, our tagged female Waveplume takes to the skies once more, her wings stretching wide as she glides effortlessly alongside the Alpha Waveplume. They soar over the vibrant mating grounds, the shoreline glimmering below, as the journey spans a breathtaking fifteen miles and takes approximately thirty minutes. As they navigate the air currents, both females call back to their nests, their melodious cries echoing across the winds, reassuring their young that they are on their way home.

Meanwhile, deep within the nest, the egg continues to crack, the sounds of life growing more pronounced with each passing moment, heralding the imminent arrival of a new chick. As the tagged female Waveplume glides back toward her nest, she embodies a grace that is both mesmerising and commanding. With a remarkable wingspan of 290 cm, she descends with the poise of a masterful aviator, landing a few feet away with an elegance that belies the urgency of the moment. Her keen eyes quickly survey the scene before her, falling upon her mate, who remains blissfully engrossed in feeding their chick, utterly oblivious to the wonders unfolding nearby.

Yet, her attention is soon captured by unmistakable signs of the egg's impending hatching. Cracks have formed across its delicate shell, accompanied by the enthusiastic sounds of life echoing from within—a jubilant cacophony that signals a momentous event is at hand. In an instant, a powerful rush of maternal instinct surges through her. Turning sharply toward her mate, she unleashes a series of urgent calls, a vocal reprimand that echoes through the air. With a sudden and dramatic flourish, she deploys her formidable wings in a swift motion, sending him tumbling from the nest with surprising force.

The impact, akin to a playful slapstick moment in nature, knocks him to the ground below, where he momentarily loses around 10% HP. Her passionate cries resonate with the urgency of the occasion, reminding him that every precious moment in their young family's life demands attention. Still nursing the sting of his recent chastisement, the male Waveplume ascends into the air, his wings flapping with a mixture of frustration and reluctant retreat. With resolute determination, he flies five miles out to sea, a careful distance that allows him to grant his mate the space she so clearly demands, while remaining vigilant over their precious nest. As he settles upon a small sandbar, a solitary haven amidst the endless azure, the gentle lapping of waves provides a soothing backdrop. Here, he finds a momentary refuge, the warm grains of sand cradling his feet as he prepares to spend hours in quiet contemplation, casting occasional glances back toward the distant shore.

With meticulous care, he preens his feathers, smoothing each plume as a way to calm his mind. Nearby, the rhythmic sound of the surf seems to offer reassurance. He forages along the bar's edge, discovering small morsels of food—tiny crustaceans and bits of seaweed—adding up to around 15 calories. Each bite not only nourishes him but also serves as a reminder of the abundance of their coastal home. In this tranquil setting, he reflects on how best to reclaim his place in their harmonious family, hoping to return with a gesture that would mend the rift between them.

An hour later, the tagged male Waveplume has taken to the air, searching for sustenance to appease his mate and restore harmony, blissfully unaware of the momentous events unfolding in the nest below. From his lofty vantage point, he casts a thoughtful gaze over the shimmering waters, preoccupied with foraging. Inside the nest, however, the smallest of the two remaining eggs rests delicately among the soft nesting materials, its fragile surface adorned with tiny cracks that trace the contours of new life. Within this fragile shell, a determined chick, brimming with energy, pecks vigorously, each rhythmic sound resonating with the promise of emergence.

The mother Waveplume stands watch, her keen eyes locked onto the egg, embodying the very essence of maternal vigilance. Anticipation fills the air as the unhatched chick instinctively senses the urgency of its arrival, its small body trembling with excitement. Together, they await the joyous moment when the egg finally yields, heralding the continuation of their family and the dawn of new adventures in their vast coastal realm, a testament to the cycles of life in the wild.

As the male Waveplume glides gracefully above the glistening surface of the ocean, his keen eyes scan the waters for a suitable offering to appease his mate. In this rich tapestry of the coastal ecosystem, he searches diligently, knowing that finding the perfect morsel is essential to restoring balance after their earlier discord. Suddenly, something unusual catches his eye—a radiant pearl, suspended in the water, gently bobbing with the currents. With a swift dive, he plunges beneath the surface, his powerful wings propelling him forward. He positions himself to grasp the pearl, seizing it with the same deftness as a catch from the sea.

This magnificent treasure, once expelled by an Animara known as Clamora, is incredibly rare and nearly extinct, making it a true marvel of the deep. These pearls, shrouded in mystery, are considered extraordinary finds by all aquatic Animara, whether they dwell in the sea or traverse both air and water. Researchers have discovered that these precious orbs contain what can only be described as condensed experience points (XP), and when cracked open, they release a radiant energy that spreads across the vicinity, benefiting all creatures nearby.

Animara researchers believe this energy expels around 1000 XP minimum. With the precious pearl securely clutched in his beak, the male Waveplume ascends from the depths, his heart soaring as he glides back toward the nest. The sun glints off the ocean's surface, illuminating the magnificent treasure he carries—a token of reconciliation meant to restore harmony with his mate.

As he approaches their home, however, an unexpected sight unfolds before him. He lands softly at the nest, only to be greeted by a cacophony of gentle chirps. To his astonishment, another of their eggs had hatched in his absence, nestled among the soft bedding alongside the small chick he had left behind. The mother Waveplume preens the newly arrived chick with tender care, her eyes gleaming with what can only be described as maternal pride.

Chapter Thirty-Four: The Family Unit

The sight of the new Gulltide chick, delicate and full of life, works wonders in alleviating any lingering tension between the parents. In this moment, all grievances seem to fade into the background, replaced by an overwhelming instinct to nurture and protect.

With a gentle nudge, the male Waveplume places the gleaming pearl in the nest, its lustrous surface catching the light in a dazzling display. Yet, neither parent pays much attention to this rare gift; their eyes are solely focused on their growing family.

Together, they begin to preen their chicks, their movements synchronised in a tender dance of parental devotion. It is a sight that echoes the nurturing bonds observed in the human world; the arrival of a newborn can mend even the deepest of wounds. As the parents express their love through gentle touches and soothing calls, they embrace the joy of their expanding family, forging a stronger connection that will carry them through the challenges that lie ahead in their coastal sanctuary.

Three weeks have passed since the Gulltide chicks first hatched, their fragile forms tucked safely into the rocky embrace of the Pinnacle Perch. What were once helpless, downy creatures have undergone a breathtaking transformation. Cloaked in juvenile feathers, their small bodies seem to hum with potential. The first tentative flutters of their wings, once feeble and uncertain, now grow stronger each day. Though they remain anchored to the safety of their lofty nest, they inch ever closer to its edge, gazing out in wide-eyed wonder at the vast, rugged coastal expanse that will soon become their domain.

The shoreline below, wild and unrelenting, stretches out as far as the eye can see. Its weathered rocks stand as ancient sentinels, polished smooth by the relentless ebb and flow of the sea. In the distance, the surf crashes against the beach, its foam sparkling in the light of a weakening sun.

Here, in the sanctuary of the coast, lies a crucial part of the Gulltides' world: the nearby mating grounds. These wide, sandy beaches are a sacred place for the Gulltides and many other Animara species. It is where new life begins. Each spring, the shores are alive with the ritualistic dance of courtship, as pairs of Gulltides reunite to begin the next cycle of life. Now, in the early days of autumn, the beaches lie quiet, a reminder of what has been and what is yet to come.

During these vital early weeks, the chicks' rapid growth is fueled by the unwavering dedication of their parents. From dawn until dusk, the adult Gulltides glide over the shoreline, returning tirelessly with fish and small sea creatures to feed their growing brood. The chicks, ravenous and demanding, consume nearly 3,850 calories in these three weeks, their bodies expanding with each meal. Their wings grow stronger, preparing for the day when they will leave the safety of the nest and take to the skies for the first time. That moment, however, is still to come.

For now, despite their growing strength, the chicks remain bound by nature's careful design. Their levels are capped at Level 1, their XP frozen for the first three months of life, allowing them to focus purely on their physical development. Though their feathers have thickened, their bodies are still vulnerable, and their parents' protection remains essential.

Predators lurk near the cliffs, their sharp eyes trained on the vulnerable young. But here, within the safety of the Pinnacle Perch, the chicks are sheltered from the many dangers that circle below. As they gather the strength and courage for their first flight, the world beyond the nest waits.

As the season ticks away, day by day, the moment draws near when our tagged Waveplumes will begin the delicate task of teaching their three Gulltide chicks the art of flight. Nestled at the base of the small rocky outcrop known as the Pinnacle Perch, the chicks have watched the sky above with growing curiosity. Soon, the adult Waveplumes will lead them to the open ground, wings spread wide, demonstrating how to catch the coastal winds that sweep through the terrain.

The first lesson is one of trust—trust in the wind, and trust in their own growing instincts. With gentle nudges and patient calls, the parents will encourage their chicks to take that first daring leap into the air. Their initial attempts will be awkward, wings flapping unsteadily, but under the watchful guidance of the Waveplumes, they will learn to glide with the currents, mastering the unseen forces that will carry them through life as creatures of the air.

Although our focus remains on the tagged Waveplume family, other Gulltide families across the mating grounds are also preparing for their first flights. Each day, the atmosphere around Pinnacle Perch hums with mounting anticipation. The Gulltide chicks, no longer content to remain nestled in the safety of their rocky home, are filled with restless energy. Their once timid movements have become deliberate; wings stretch and flap as they imitate their parents' graceful mastery of the air. They watch intently as the adult Waveplumes soar above the cliffs, navigating the coastal winds with effortless precision, their hearts yearning to ride those same currents.

On the ground, the chicks practice diligently, their small wings beating furiously as they feel the slightest whisper of lift beneath them. They hop and flutter along the rocky terrain, clumsy and awkward, yet bursting with promise. The excitement among them is palpable; every gust of wind that sweeps through the nest seems to urge them onward, inviting them to take that first leap into the vast unknown.

Yet, the time is not quite right. The parents remain vigilant, aware of the delicate balance between eagerness and readiness. They observe their chicks with a keen eye, understanding that while the desire to fly is present, the necessary skills have not yet fully developed. The lessons of flight cannot be rushed, and so the days tick by, each one bringing the chicks closer to that pivotal moment. The wind, the sky, and the world beyond their nest await them—soon, they too will soar.

Chapter Thirty-Five: Wings Of The Young

As dawn breaks over the salt marsh, the air is thick with anticipation. Today, three young Gulltide chicks stand on the verge of a life-defining moment—their first flight.

For weeks, they have watched from the safety of their nest as their parents soared high above, mastering the winds with elegant ease. Now, their time has come. Their parents circle overhead, their expansive wings spanning over 1.5 metres (4.92 feet), casting protective shadows over the marshlands. Their calls are soft yet insistent, urging the fledglings to trust the instincts that have been stirring inside them.

Below, the chicks spread their wings for the first time, their wingspans measuring around 0.8 metres (2.62 feet). The wind teases their feathers, sending a ripple of excitement and trepidation through their small bodies. It's a sensation they've felt before, but never like this—now, the wind offers more than just comfort. It promises freedom. Their parents glide gracefully above, demonstrating what lies ahead, urging the chicks to take that final step into the unknown. The eldest chick steps forward, its wings trembling slightly as it balances on the nest's edge. A gust of wind lifts it briefly, giving a fleeting taste of what's to come. The others follow, inching closer to the precipice, eyes locked on the skies above. Their tiny hearts race, and with one last glance at their parents, they leap.

With a flurry of uncertain wingbeats, the three Gulltide chicks embark on their first tentative flights, flapping and gliding in three short, five-foot circles directly above the nest. Their wings, still new to the sensation of air beneath them, carry them low over the grasses in bursts that last around ten minutes. Each movement is a blend of effort and discovery, as they cautiously test the limits of their young bodies, feeling the lift and pull of the wind for the first time. Their flight is far from graceful, but there is no mistaking the significance of this moment—these are the first true steps toward mastering the skies.

Though they remain close to the nest, each chick demonstrates a spark of independence, a growing confidence with every circuit. They flap awkwardly at first, then glide, as if trying to understand the balance between effort and ease. Their movements are still rough, yet each pass strengthens their wings and sharpens their instincts. Above them, the parents soar with quiet pride, their watchful presence offering reassurance as their offspring test the air.

For the parents, this is a moment of both joy and vigilance. While they remain ready to intervene if danger arises, they allow the chicks this freedom, knowing that these early flights are vital to their development. Soon, the chicks will be ready to leave the safety of the nest and explore the wider world. But for now, they practise in short, careful circles, preparing themselves for the adventures to come. As they continue these first steps into the sky, we shall take a closer look at their stats, as their wings grow stronger with each burst of flight.

Animara Metrics Table			
	Chick 1	Chick 2	Chick 3
HP Score	90%	88%	92%
Total Flight Time	30 Minutes	30 Minutes	30 Minutes
Distance Travelled	15 Feet	15 Feet	15 Feet
Calories Consumed	150 Cal	165 Cal	155 Cal
XP Score	160 XP	150 XP	165 XP
XP Needed For Next Level	N/A Level Cap In Place	N/A Level Cap In Place	N/A Level Cap In Place

As dawn breaks, illuminating the tranquil landscape, a new day dawns for the young Gulltide chicks.

Today, they will not venture far from the nest; instead, their attentive parents will guide them in mastering the art of flight. With the sun rising higher, the chicks will practise their skills, gradually gaining altitude as they circle in their familiar five-foot arcs. Under the watchful eyes of their parents, they will ascend a few metres higher with each circuit, learning to harness the air currents that lift them skyward.

This gradual elevation, repeated several times throughout the day, transforms their once timid flaps into confident strokes. By day's end, they will have soared to an impressive height of approximately twenty metres above the ground. Each ascent marks a significant milestone in their development as they embrace the exhilaration of flight, inching ever closer to the freedom of the skies that await them.

As the sun sets on another day of practice, the mother Gulltide encourages her chicks to leave the safety of their familiar circular flight path around the nest. With each gentle call, she instilled a sense of adventure, urging them to stretch their wings and explore the world beyond their secure haven. Yet, despite her coaxing, the chicks hesitate, their instincts tethered to the safety of the small space they know so well.

It isn't until the tagged male Waveplume gracefully lands nearby that the atmosphere shifts. Sensing the moment, the mother Gulltide calls out to her partner, and together they form a united front. With a series of encouraging calls and a few confident flaps, the Waveplume joins the mother in enticing the chicks to follow them. Feeling the gentle push of their parents' presence, the young ones finally muster the courage to break away from their safe, small circle.

With their parents leading the way, they venture outward, soaring toward the expansive marsh. Each flap of their wings carries a mix of excitement and trepidation as they embrace this thrilling new chapter, ready to discover the vast skies that await them beyond the nest. The next day dawns with an uneasy stillness, the warning call from the previous evening still echoing in the mind.

The mother Gulltide senses the lingering tension among the flock and recognizes the need to prepare her chicks for the skies while remaining vigilant. Rather than encourage them to take to the air just yet, she focuses on teaching them essential flight behaviours right there on the ground. With calm determination, she demonstrates the mechanics of flapping their wings, showcasing the nuances of takeoffs and landings. Each movement is deliberate and practised, instilling in her fledglings the vital skills they will need when the time comes to soar.

Interestingly, Animara researchers have discovered that it is the female Waveplumes who excel as the better teachers and flyers. Their graceful manoeuvres and patient guidance play a crucial role in the chicks' development. In contrast, the male Waveplumes, while less adept at teaching, shine in their abilities to battle and defend against threats, their robust physiques well-suited for combat. Meanwhile, the tagged male Waveplume, aware of the potential danger that still looms nearby, joins the Alpha Waveplume in a strategic meeting. Together, they scan the horizon, their keen eyes searching for signs of danger that may threaten the safety of the flock. As the mother instilled confidence in her young ones, the male and Alpha remained vigilant, their alertness heightened.

The lessons of the day are marked by an instinctual understanding of survival; while the mother prepares her chicks for eventual flight, the tagged Waveplume father and Alpha Waveplume collaborate to uncover the unseen menace, ensuring the safety of not only their own families but also that of the entire flock. This vital responsibility falls on the shoulders of the Waveplume males during the mating season, and it is one of the reasons Gulltides hold Waveplume males in such high esteem.

Chapter Thirty-Six: A Father's Teachings

It has been several days since the young Waveplumes, now known as Gulltides, first ventured beyond the safety of their nest. With tentative flutters, they stretched their wings, tasting freedom for the first time. Their parents, vigilant and ever-watchful, guide them through this delicate phase. Each flight is brief and unsteady, but vital. The chicks teeter through the air, their feathers catching the wind as they struggle to remain aloft. The parents circle above, offering soft calls of encouragement. The marsh below awaits them, but for now, every flight is a small triumph, a step toward independence.

Under the watchful eyes of their ever-attentive parents, they have made remarkable progress. The once timid flights around their hummock have transformed into confident laps, their wings gaining strength with each graceful beat. Thanks to careful nurturing, these young ones have grown significantly—both in experience and in energy.

Each has amassed an additional 200 XP, a vital boost for their development, while their caloric intake has tripled, providing the fuel necessary for more ambitious ventures. Their flight paths now extend up to three miles from the nest, a small but commendable improvement in such a short time. As they glide across the mating grounds, there is little doubt that these fledglings are well on their way to mastering the skies.

Despite their newfound strength and growing confidence, a subtle unease has settled over the young Gulltides. Their once carefree flights, though longer and more assured, are now punctuated by moments of hesitation, as if they too can sense something amiss. Each beat of their wings carries them further from the safety of the nest, but with every mile, a strange tension follows. The mating grounds, once bustling with life and calls of the Gulltides, are growing quieter with each passing day. As more couples depart with their chicks in tow, the landscape becomes eerily still, the familiar sounds fading into silence.

The fledglings, though inexperienced, seem attuned to this shift. They pause more often, their bright eyes scanning the skies and grounds below, as if searching for an unseen presence. Though no danger has appeared, the quiet departure of others stirs an instinctual caution—a subtle warning that their world is changing. Sensing the shift in the air, our tagged male Waveplume, ever vigilant, takes his fatherly duties to the next level. The once relaxed guardianship now gives way to purposeful action as he gathers his chicks beneath his wing, their small forms huddling close for reassurance.

With quiet determination, he begins teaching them how to harness their natural abilities—moves that will soon be essential for their survival. The first lesson is Air Cutter. With a sharp, controlled flap of his wings, he demonstrates the precision needed to slice through the air, sending a sharp gust toward a nearby hummock. The chicks watch intently, mimicking his movements, their tentative attempts slowly gaining power.

Meanwhile, the tagged female ventures further afield, foraging for food not just for her brood, but for the elder Gulltide still lingering at the mating grounds. Her forays are swift, yet calculated, as she too senses the tension in the air.

Under a growing sense of unease, our tagged Waveplume instinctively prepares his young Gulltides for the unknown. The once-thriving mating grounds are now quiet, and though no immediate threat has appeared, the weight of the unpredictable hangs in the air. To safeguard his offspring, he takes it upon himself to ensure they are ready for any challenge. Their survival depends on mastering the basics. He begins with the Breeze Attack—a simple yet powerful move, where a controlled flap of the wings channels air to disrupt nearby threats. The young Gulltides, eager but awkward, mimic their father's movements. Each attempt is a mix of clumsy determination and budding skill, their fledgling wings struggling to find the right rhythm. Yet with each flap, they grow stronger, more coordinated, and their grasp of the technique deepens.

Our tagged male Waveplume circles above, vigilant, offering encouragement with soft calls. He knows these skills, though simple now, may one day be crucial for their survival. Every moment spent honing their abilities is another step toward independence, another layer of protection against the unpredictable world that awaits them.

But defence is just as crucial. He then demonstrates the Feather Shield—a basic but vital move. By bracing their wings, the chicks create a protective barrier with their feathers, shielding themselves from sudden danger. Though rudimentary, it provides immediate security, and with each practice, the young Gulltides learn to brace against the unexpected.

Next, he introduces the Squirt Shot, a clever technique that draws moisture from the marsh and air, turning it into small, sharp bursts of water. This move is intended to ward off predators or rivals. To make the lessons engaging, he encourages his chicks to aim at clusters of reeds and rocks scattered around the marsh. Each successful hit earns them a satisfying 5 XP, turning training into an exciting game.

As the Gulltides practice diligently, their precision improves, and their cooperation strengthens. They learn that survival relies not just on strength but on skill and unity. With every movement taught, our tagged Waveplume's guidance ensures that these young Gulltides are not merely playing, but training to become formidable creatures, ready to face the world beyond the safety of their nest. Each move, each successful attack, transforms them from dependent chicks into capable fledglings, ingraining the instincts they will need to thrive in the unpredictable world ahead.

As the young Gulltide chicks revel in their newfound skills, their exuberance fills the air with a delightful chorus of chirps. They dive and swoop, their fledgling wings flapping in a joyous display of youthful energy. However, this moment of innocence is abruptly shattered when our tagged Waveplume hears the distant calls of the flock—urgent and resonant, echoing a familiar warning. A threat has been sensed before, an unseen danger lurking just beyond the marshlands, casting a shadow over their playful frolicking.

Without hesitation, he commands his chicks to follow him, the instinct to protect igniting within him. With a swift flap of his wings, he leads them in a short but determined flight back to the haven of their nest. The chicks, now more agile and coordinated from their training, keep pace with their father, instinctively weaving through the air as they navigate the familiar landscape. As they soar, they feel the exhilarating rush of the wind beneath their wings, a taste of freedom that deepens their bond. The comforting sight of their mother and the elder Gulltide waiting anxiously in the nest draws nearer, a reassuring presence amid the uncertainty. With the spectre of danger still looming, the safe embrace of home beckons, offering solace from the invisible threats of the world beyond.

No sooner had the tagged male Waveplume delivered his chicks safely back to the nest than he was airborne once more, his instincts driving him to confront the encroaching danger. With powerful strokes of his wings, he ascends into the sky, joining forces with the Alpha Waveplume. Together, they soar over the expansive mating grounds and its surrounding marshlands, their sharp eyes scanning the horizon for any signs of threat.

The air is thick with tension as they glide through the sky, the rhythm of their wings synchronised in a determined dance of vigilance. Below them, the landscape unfolds, a vibrant tapestry of reeds and shallow waters, each ripple concealing the unknown.

Chapter Thirty-Seven: A Cloud Of Chaos

The Alpha Waveplume leads the way, his every movement a testament to his years of experience and innate authority. His wings, weathered but powerful, sweep through the salt-laden air with deliberate grace, guiding the flock along the familiar paths.

Behind him, our tagged Waveplume follows closely, keenly observing every motion, every signal. He is an apprentice in every sense, learning not only the physical demands of the watch but also the subtleties of leadership and vigilance. The Alpha communicates with the barest of gestures—a tilt of the head, a shift in the wind beneath his wings—and our tagged Waveplume responds, their unspoken language honed through shared responsibility.

It is not merely the passing of time, but the growing bond between them that strengthens their determination. In the moments when the flock rests, and the vast horizon is theirs to guard, the two males share an understanding—each vigilant for the safety of their kin. Their bond is forged not in the face of danger alone but in the quiet spaces between, where trust and responsibility intertwine. Every call, every swoop through the air, is a reaffirmation of their shared purpose: to protect the flock and their precious territory from unseen threats.

For hours, the pair of male Waveplumes glided along in near silence, wings outstretched as they completed three full circuits over the vast mating grounds. From the shimmering coastline to the sprawling salt marshes, their keen eyes had scanned the forty-three-mile length and fifteen-mile breadth of the territory.

Their ability to remain airborne for such long stretches reflected not only their endurance but also their unwavering commitment to safeguarding the flock. Using the wind currents to conserve energy, they had tirelessly searched for the threat that had disturbed the flock's fragile peace. Now, after three circuits, fatigue was beginning to creep in. But just as the weight of their long flight started to take its toll, their mates appeared.

Rising gracefully from the ground, the females soared up to meet them, bringing much-needed nourishment mid-flight. Each carried what she could—small chunks of Mackerlure, scraps of dried seaweed—whatever could sustain their mates during their watch. In a seamless and precise exchange, the females matched their males' speed, passing the food with a swift dip of their beaks as they flew alongside.

Instead of returning immediately to their nests, the females joined their mates, flying together for two more circuits of the mating grounds. The sky was theirs, and for a time, they shared the burden of vigilance. Only after these rounds did the females peel away, descending gracefully toward the marsh and leaving the males to continue their relentless patrol of the vast expanse below. The quiet connection between them, sustained by their shared purpose, ensured the safety of their territory and kin.

Halfway through a circuit of their vast mating grounds, the Waveplume males glide with fluid precision. Below them, the rugged beach stretches wide—a patchwork of rocky outcrops, tidal pools brimming with life, and sand streaked with seaweed.

At the heart of this landscape stands the Pinnacle Perch, a towering stone formation, its smooth surface polished by centuries of wind and water. As they sail over the coastline, their wings nearly motionless, a sudden explosion of dirt, sand, and seaweed erupts from the earth, tearing through the peaceful scene below.

The Alpha's keen eyes lock onto the disturbance immediately. In an instant, he and his companion break their glide, ascending sharply into the air with wings beating in perfect unison. Higher and higher they climb, scanning the scene below with focused intensity.

Then, in perfect synchronicity, they dive. Arcing gracefully through the sky, their forms cut a wide path as they sweep toward the source of the explosion. The tranquil circuit of the mating grounds is now charged with sudden urgency.

The Waveplumes respond instinctively, their flight a perfect expression of nature's power and grace as they descend toward the chaos, prepared to defend their territory and restore the delicate balance that has been shattered. As the male Waveplume guardians fly closer to the chaotic plume of debris at the edge of their mating grounds, their evolved eyes, honed by nature, discern movement within the swirling cloud.

Amidst the tumbling sand and scattered seaweed, one silhouette stands out—a familiar sight of a Gulltide, its wings spread wide in a desperate attempt to shield itself from the onslaught. The guardians' hearts quicken, recognizing the unmistakable form of their kin amidst the chaos. Yet, the other two silhouettes remain harder to discern, flickering in and out of focus as they shift through the debris.

Tension hangs in the air, thick with urgency, as the guardians realise the Gulltide is in distress, calling out for aid against the encroaching threat. In that moment, a powerful instinct surges through their bodies, igniting a fierce protective drive.

Undeterred by the surrounding tumult, they unleash a torrent of water from their beaks—a brilliant cascade that arcs through the air, shattering the dust cloud. The force of the spray creates a shimmering hole in the chaos, revealing the trembling form of the Gulltide. With a swift and practised motion, the guardians cease their watery assault and descend, landing with precision in front of the Gulltide.

Their vibrant plumage stands out starkly against the muted colours of the debris, forming a formidable barrier between their kin and the two ominous shapes lurking within the cloud. With wings poised and eyes narrowed in determination, the Waveplume guardians stand resolute, their powerful presence radiating an unyielding sense of courage. Every instinct urges them to protect, ready to confront the impending threat and defend their flock members against the danger that looms in the shadows. As the dust settles, the two Waveplume protectors find themselves face to face with a hulking Craghorn, its boulder-like skin gleaming menacingly in the fading light.

This formidable Rock-type Animara looms over them, radiating an aura of raw power that sends a chill through the air. Tension crackles like electricity, and the guardians brace themselves for the impending confrontation In this moment, they stand as sentinels against an overwhelming threat, an Animara Trainer lurking ominously behind its Craghorn, ready to unleash chaos.

A quick glance at the stat tag reveals that as our tagged Waveplume is on the verge of engaging in a battle against a tamed Animara. The Craghorn stands before it, boasting a Level 6 rating, yet it harbours an elemental weakness that might suggest an advantage for the Waveplume. However, in the intricate dance of Animara battles, elemental weaknesses are seldom definitive. Each encounter is a testament to resilience and strategy, where the tide can turn in an instant, defying the odds.

On the edge of the mating grounds, where the waves crash violently against the rocky coastline, an electric tension fills the air as both sides prepare to strike. The trainer of the Craghorn, eyes sharp with determination, senses the pivotal moment. With a swift command, the sturdy creature lunges forward, unleashing a powerful Rock Shatter that sends a jagged boulder hurtling through the air, striking the Alpha Waveplume with fierce precision.

In an impressive display of agility, the majestic Alpha Waveplume retaliates, unleashing a torrential blast of water in a desperate attempt to drench the Craghorn and hinder its movements. Yet, the nimble Craghorn deftly sidesteps the oncoming deluge, closing the distance with relentless speed. With a thunderous Stone Cascade, the Craghorn sends a barrage of stones crashing down upon the Alpha Waveplume, sending it sprawling against the rocky shore. The vibrant feathers of the Alpha Waveplume ruffle violently in the aftermath, signalling its defeat.

The Craghorn's trainer, pulse racing with adrenaline, watches intently. In a heartbeat, they seize their moment and, with a swift flick of the wrist, the Capture Card hurtles toward the Alpha Waveplume, its fate hanging precariously in the balance.

Chapter Thirty-Eight: Passing The Baton

In a heartbeat, our tagged Waveplume responds, wings flashing through the air to deflect the capture card destined for the Alpha. The impact sends the device spiralling harmlessly away, but the Waveplume's actions are far from over. With a mighty beat of its wings, it draws upon the environment itself—summoning a tremendous gust that sweeps across the rocky shoreline.

Water sprays from the nearby pools, mixing with sand and debris, turning the air into a whirling storm of elements. Rocks, driftwood, and seawater hurtle toward the unsuspecting Craghorn, striking with the full force of nature. The Craghorn staggers, its once-imposing figure now struggling to stay upright against the onslaught.

The Alpha, ever watchful, senses the change. In a rare display of humility, it steps back, allowing the younger Waveplume to rise to the fore. This is no longer its battle to lead. The mantle has passed, and the young bird, eyes sharp with determination, stands resolute at the heart of the storm. As the debris settles and the Craghorn reels from the assault, the balance of power shifts, and it is clear that this new generation is more than ready to face the challenges that lie ahead.

The tagged Waveplume stands firm on the rocky terrain, wings partially spread, its sharp eyes fixed on the trainer's Craghorn. Both Animara are locked in a tense standoff, waiting for the first move.

"Craghorn, Venom Strike!" the trainer commands. The Craghorn surges forward, horn glowing with toxic energy as it charges.

Just as Craghorn lunges, the Waveplume reacts. With a powerful beat of its wings, it lifts into the air a few feet, evading the strike with graceful ease. The Venom Strike hits empty ground as the Waveplume hovers, its keen eyes scanning for the next opportunity.

The Waveplume opens its beak wide, gathering moisture from the air, and unleashes a massive Water Cannon. A concentrated jet of water blasts toward the Craghorn, soaking it and knocking it back. Water splashes off the rocky hide, glistening in the sunlight as the Craghorn shakes off the attack.

"Craghorn, Rock Blaster!" the trainer shouts.

The Craghorn leaps and fires a stream of pebbles and stones toward the Waveplume. But the tagged Waveplume is too quick, rising just beyond reach as the projectiles scatter harmlessly beneath it. Now hovering, the Waveplume beats its wings harder, summoning a powerful gust of wind that sends debris swirling around. With a fierce cry, it channels the gust, creating a small cyclone that rushes toward the Craghorn. The winds roar to life, trapping the Craghorn in a whirlwind of feathers and air. Craghorn struggles against the storm, but the sheer force overwhelms it, sending it tumbling to the ground.

As the dust settles and Craghorn lies still, the trainer's heart races. Realising the battle is lost, they quickly pull out a capture card, anxiety etched across their face. With a swift motion, they activate the device, and a beam of light envelops the fallen Animara. In an instant, the Craghorn is drawn back into the capture card, the glow fading as it seals away the defeated Animara.

Without wasting another moment, the trainer turns on their heel and makes a desperate run for safety, their pulse pounding in their ears as they navigate the rocky terrain, eager to put distance between themselves and the victorious Waveplume.

It is a sad truth that humans, with all their ingenuity and ambition, are sometimes the greatest threat to the very creatures they admire. Here, on this reserve, the Animara thrive in their natural environment, unburdened by the demands of the outside world. Yet, there are those who see them not as magnificent beings to be respected, but as tools to be exploited. Trainers, desperate to gain an edge in the competitive leagues, will go to alarming lengths to capture what they deem the finest Animara.

In this case, we witnessed the unsettling reality of poaching in action—a trainer, disregarding the sanctity of the reserve, attempting to steal one of its most cherished inhabitants. Today, the target was our Gulltide flock. These birds are integral to the delicate balance of this ecosystem. Yet, to the poacher's eye, they are seen only as potential assets, not as Animara that embody the very essence of this protected place. The hunt, the disruption, and the threat to their nesting grounds have left the flock in a state of distress, their peaceful existence shattered. It is a sobering reminder of the lengths some will go to, and the cost it imposes on the natural world.

The battle-weary Waveplumes, wings tattered and heavy, glide in silence across the skies, their graceful forms casting shadows over the coastline below. With each strained beat, they edge closer to the familiar rock formation that serves as their sanctuary, Pinnacle Perch. The elder of the two, the Alpha, glances briefly at his younger counterpart—a gesture so subtle it could be missed, yet laden with meaning. There is no need for elaborate displays; a simple tilt of his head speaks volumes. It is as though, in that fleeting moment, the Alpha acknowledges the strength and resolve of his fellow, granting an unspoken permission, an invitation, to someday soon fly solo.

Our younger Waveplume, though battered, holds steady, sensing the quiet respect. Together, they descend toward the Perch, where the battles of the day slowly give way to the quietude of the sea and their respective family units. As we shift our focus to the younger pair of tagged Waveplumes, the female begins her delicate work, tending to her mate with a grace that speaks of love and loyalty. She carefully preens his ragged feathers, smoothing each one as if to erase the scars of battle. With gentle nudges, she tends to his wings, mending what she can while letting her soft murmurs calm his spirit.

Nearby, their chicks sleep soundly, nestled together beneath the soft down of the nest, their tiny breaths steady and rhythmic, unaware of the care being lavished just beside them. While her mate rests, exhausted from the trials of the day, she remains vigilant, her keen eyes scanning the horizon.

Yet, even in this moment of watchfulness, her movements are tender. She will shield him from the night's cold, wrapping her body close to his, providing warmth and solace. As the chicks stir in their sleep, still safe under her protective wing, she knows their time in the nest is nearing its end, but for now, her focus is on restoring her mate, ensuring he is ready for the journey ahead.

As dawn breaks over the salt marsh, a soft light brushes the feathers of the tagged male Waveplume, still resting in the nest. His injuries, though not life-threatening, carry the weight of his struggle against the Craghorn, leaving him weakened and grounded. His mate, always vigilant, senses his need. On most mornings, she would tend to their chicks, but today her priorities have shifted. With a lingering glance at her mate and their slumbering young, she rises into the air, her wings catching the first rays of dawn.

As she glides from the nest, the subtle awareness of being watched settles around her. The eyes of the younger Gulltide mothers—whom she had aided in their moments of need—follow her movement, silent and expectant. She flies with purpose, scanning the marsh below for clusters of berries and healing plants to speed her mate's recovery. The pull between nurturing her young and tending to her partner tugs at her, but she trusts the flock. The elder Gulltide, alongside others, will keep watch over the chicks in her absence.

The air feels different this morning, as if a shared understanding ripples through the flock. Each bird seems to sense an impending change, though none give voice to it. For now, the female's focus is singular—gathering the nourishment her mate requires so that, together, they can face whatever lies ahead.

Chapter Thirty-Nine : Tidal Games

As the soft light of a spring morning spreads over the marsh, our tagged avian family stirs. The air is cool but fragrant with the scent of fresh blooms, a reminder that the season of renewal is in full swing. Our tagged Waveplume parents wake first, stretching their wings and shaking off the dew that clings to their feathers. Their sharp eyes scan the horizon, already calculating the day ahead. Today will be their last here, and every moment counts. The chicks begin to rouse, their small bodies still clumsy with sleep, wings twitching in anticipation.

The tagged mother takes to the skies first, her wings slicing through the morning air as she makes her way to the food cache. Below, the father keeps a watchful eye on their young, encouraging them with soft calls to rise and prepare for the day. The chicks chirp in response, their excitement growing as they await the return of their mother. Moments later, she glides back, a bounty of nuts and ripe fruits clasped in her beak. Landing gracefully beside them, she begins the crucial task of feeding each chick, carefully ensuring they each receive 150 calories.

With gentle persistence, she breaks the food into manageable pieces, offering a mix of rich walnuts and succulent berries, providing the nourishment they need for the challenging day ahead. As the chicks devour their meals with eager beaks, the sun climbs higher, casting warmth over the marsh.

Just as they begin to settle after their feast, the elder Gulltide arrives, embodying the nurturing spirit of a grandmother. Her presence brings comfort and reassurance, a gentle support for both parents as they prepare for the day's endeavours. With a soft coo and a watchful eye, she joins the family, ready to help guide the chicks through their first real forage. As morning's grasp begins to take hold, casting a warm glow over the coastal landscape, the tides gently lap against the shore, ushering in a world teeming with new foraging opportunities. Our tagged chicks, now capable of sustained flight for up to thirty minutes, are poised to embrace this momentous day. \

To them, the sky is not merely a vast expanse of blue, but a vibrant playground filled with promise and excitement. As they take to the air for their inaugural forage, their parents skillfully mimic the dives and techniques essential for catching food from the ocean below. The fledglings, wide-eyed and eager, observe their every move, instinctively mirroring each deft manoeuvre as they practise their newfound skills. The father leads the way, calling softly to his young, while the mother maintains a watchful eye, ensuring her chicks remain close.

Sensing their readiness, the father encourages them to dive for real. With hearts racing and a sense of adventure in their wings, the chicks plunge toward the glistening water, but on their first attempt, none manage to catch a meal. Yet, as is the way of nature, trial and error are vital parts of life.

Regrouping, the family takes to the skies once more, flying in a graceful V-formation that optimises their energy and reduces wind resistance. The adults skillfully adjust their positions to maintain the formation, while the chicks, filled with determination, refine their flying skills and build their strength.

Together, they glide effortlessly over the tidal currents, embodying both unity and freedom as they embrace the exhilarating thrill of the chase in their vibrant coastal home. Each attempt strengthens their bond and reinforces an essential lesson: perseverance is key in the ever-challenging journey.

As our tagged chicks continue their airborne ballet, they mimic the foraging manoeuvres of their parents and the elder Gulltides, absorbing every lesson like sponges. The parents' eyes, trained and sharp, scan the retreating tide for signs of movement—each flicker of fish beneath the surface is a potential meal.

The sky fills with the silhouettes of other Gulltide families, all united in the same quest for nourishment. The sight of these formations ignites a competitive spirit within our tagged family; a primal instinct that compels them to venture further, despite the inherent risks.

The ocean stretches before them, a vast expanse filled with both peril and promise. Their parents, keenly aware of the potential dangers, urge them onward, understanding that growth often requires a leap of faith. As the family glides further out to sea, the thrill of the chase mingles with the tension of uncertainty. It is a risky endeavour, but in the dance of survival, some risks are indeed worth taking.

As the parents meticulously scan the shimmering surface of the water below, their instincts finely honed to detect even the slightest ripple of movement, a sudden flurry of action unfolds. Having journeyed around fifteen miles in a north-easterly direction, they find themselves nearer the thermal-rich waters of the northern region of the reserve, a place teeming with life.

Our tagged female, driven by an innate urge to forage, draws her wings in close and ascends gracefully into the sky. With an elegant loop that appears almost choreographed, she positions herself perfectly for a dive. In one swift, seamless motion, she plunges into the glistening depths, disappearing beneath the surface. Minutes later, she re-emerges triumphantly, a large Tsunaflare clasped firmly in her beak.

The stat tag reveals this prize holds approximately 250 calories—ample sustenance to either store in their wet cache or have as the family's next meal. Revered historically in folklore, the Tsunaflare is celebrated in stories and songs alike, as it is adorned with crown-like fins that grace its head and body, embodying an elegance steeped in the rich traditions of the sea.

Seconds later, inspired by her success, our tagged male mimics her manoeuvre. With a calculated dive, he too returns to the surface, a second Tsunaflare captured in his beak, perfectly mirroring the caloric bounty of his mate. In this synchronised display of skill, the family strengthens their bond and ensures their survival. Their successful foraging reinforces vital lessons of teamwork and resilience, essential as they navigate the myriad challenges of their coastal habitat, where folklore dances with the tide and nature's rhythms dictate their existence.

With their calorically rich haul firmly clasped in their beaks, our tagged parents lead their family back toward the nest, a palpable sense of accomplishment radiating from their graceful forms. As they glide, the elder Gulltide takes on the role of guardian, gliding low over the ocean's surface, her watchful eyes scanning for any signs of danger. Below her, the chicks, emboldened by their recent success, begin to mimic the foraging techniques they have just observed.

However, instead of the prized Tsunaflare, they return with bits of seaweed and other ocean detritus, their playful antics a delightful sight against the backdrop of the sparkling sea. Each errant dive and playful splash is not merely a game; it is a crucial opportunity for honing their foraging skills, preparing them for the day when they, too, will embark on their own foraging adventures. In this way, the cycle of learning continues, echoing the timeless rhythms of life within this vibrant coastal ecosystem.

Chapter Forty: Ebb And Flow

A few hours have passed, and the marsh lies in serene stillness, bathed in the soft light of afternoon. The tide has retreated, revealing the rich, teeming world of the mating grounds. Rock pools glitter in the sunlight, brimming with the promise of easy foraging—small fish dart between the rocks, while crabs scuttle beneath the surface.

Yet, for now, the Waveplume family remains at rest. The chicks, utterly spent from their first foraging flight, are huddled together in the nest, their tiny bodies rising and falling with the deep, exhausted breaths of sleep.

Above them, the tagged male Waveplume stands sentinel, his sharp gaze fixed on the horizon, ever-watchful. His Sentinel Instinct is fully engaged, heightening his awareness as he guards his vulnerable young. His feathers are still dishevelled from the morning's dive, but he makes no move to preen. He will have time later. For now, he is solely focused on their safety.

The female, nearby, tends to herself, carefully removing bits of debris from her plumage. Weariness clings to her every motion, but she moves with quiet purpose.

Across the marsh, the elder Gulltide has returned to her own nest, satisfied that her grandchildren are safe for the moment.

The tide pools beckon, offering a bounty of food, but for now, the family rests, gathering strength for what remains of the day. The peaceful lull is temporary—soon, they will need to return to the task of foraging before the tides shift again, but for now, a deep and quiet weariness lingers over them.As evening rolls in, a soft glow settles over the marsh, the fading light casting long shadows across the tidal pools. The air grows cooler, and the time for rest is over.

The urgency of feeding presses upon the Waveplume parents—their chicks, still slumbering in the nest, will soon wake hungry. The tide is creeping back in, and the window to feed grows shorter.

The male Waveplume, ever vigilant, stands watch over his family, his keen eyes scanning the horizon as the light begins to fade. His feathers are still unpreened, a testament to his unwavering dedication as protector. His mate, with a graceful flick of her wings, takes to the sky. She glides effortlessly over the marsh, her flight sure and purposeful, toward their wet food cache hidden among the rocks. Earlier in the day, they had stored away an aquatic Animara, one of the larger catches, its weight promising a nourishing meal. She reaches the cache swiftly, plucking the prey from the water's edge and returning to the nest.

With practised ease, she lands beside the nest and begins to break the large Animara into smaller chunks. The chicks stir, sensing food, their hungry beaks opening wide. One by one, she feeds them, ensuring each gets their share of around 80 Calories each. She does this while her mate remains on guard, ever watchful as the day slips into night.

As dawn spreads its golden light across the coastal mating grounds, our tagged family stirs, feathers shaking off the morning dew. Today marks a pivotal moment in their lives—the day they prepare their young to embark on their first steps toward independence.

In most families, the path ahead is simple: when the brood consists of only males or only females, the chicks follow the parent of the same sex, leaving the other parent to recover and prepare for the next season. But this season has had the blessing of both, with both male and female offspring. Traditionally, this would mean the parents must split, each guiding their respective chicks on separate journeys. Yet, uncertainty lingers in the air. Will the family divide, with the father teaching the male chicks the skills needed for the open sea, while the mother tends to the females, preparing them for nesting? Or will the parents chart a new course together, guiding their young in unison?

The moment is ripe with possibility, the air thick with the unknown, as they prepare to take flight. Each chick, on the cusp of maturity, is ready to spread its wings, but their future remains undecided. Whatever path they choose, the vast sky stretches before them, filled with opportunity—and challenge.

As the morning wears on, the coastal mating grounds reveal their ever-shifting beauty. The salt marsh stretches out in a patchwork of shallow pools and wind-swept grasses, the tide inching in and out as though the land itself breathes. Sunlight glints off the water's surface, casting dancing reflections across the rocks and tidal inlets. Waves lap gently at the shoreline, smoothing stones worn down by centuries of patient tides. In the distance, jagged cliffs rise, their faces streaked with salt spray, while seabirds call overhead, carried by the sea breeze. This landscape is alive with rhythm, an endless cycle of change, where nothing remains still for long.

This restlessness extends to our tagged family, poised at the edge of their nest, readying themselves to take flight. But before they can lift off, two powerful figures descend from above—the Alpha pair, their sleek forms cutting through the sky with effortless grace. They circle the Pinnacle Perch, their sharp eyes locking onto the family below, before landing beside the nest.

A hush falls over the marsh as the Alphas' presence commands attention. With a simple, piercing call, they stop our tagged family in their tracks. The parents freeze, their wings half-extended, recognizing the signal instantly.

The Alphas intervene for reasons known only to them. Perhaps the time isn't right, or perhaps they see something our family does not. The marsh, alive with motion only moments ago, now feels suspended, as if nature itself has paused to listen, waiting for the next moment to unfold. The air is still, a quiet tension hanging over the mating grounds, until the Alpha Waveplumes, standing at the base of the Pinnacle Perch beside our tagged family's nest, let out a long, melodic flute-like call. The sound sweeps across the landscape, echoing over the rock pools and stony shore, commanding the attention of the entire flock. It is more than just a call—it is a signal of leadership. All eyes turn to the Alpha pair, their voices resonating with purpose. This moment marks the readiness of our tagged parents, not only to care for their own young, but to take on the mantle of guiding their flock.

The call is rich and full, a stirring message of responsibility. As the Alphas let out another series of melodic calls, the flock listens intently, almost as if the question is being asked: who will go with our family as they begin their own journey and start a new flock?

For a moment, there is total silence across the entire flock. Not a feather stirs, the air thick with anticipation, as though the entire colony is holding its breath. Then, softly at first, melodic trumpet-like calls filter back, echoing across the salt marsh. The first responses come from the Gulltide couples hidden among the reeds, their voices resonant and sure. One by one, almost every bonded pair from the marsh responds — forty in total.

Their calls rise in perfect harmony, a collective answer to the Alpha's summons. The sound ripples outward, gathering strength as it spreads, washing over the flock like a wave. Soon, another thirty bonded pairs scattered along the coastline add their voices, filling the air with their melodic replies until the chorus finally reaches the Alphas at the base of the Pinnacle Perch.

In total, seventy bonded pairs, along with their young, will follow our tagged family. When the morning sun rises, the flock will split, guided by the leadership of the tagged male as he leads them on a new journey. Though the flock will divide, it is not a true separation, but an expansion of their legacy. The two groups will remain linked, sharing the same ancient foraging routes and continuing to support each other when needed. Just as human families maintain strong bonds despite great distances, the Gulltides are united by deep ties.

For them, the flock is everything. Even when miles apart, they will remain connected, their shared history and kinship ensuring that they always come to each other's aid. In the morning light, as one flock becomes two, it is not an end but a new beginning — one that carries the promise of independence while holding fast to the strength of family.

Chapter Forty-One: Coastal Congregation

As twilight descends upon the mating grounds, the new flock of Gulltides encircles the nest of the tagged Waveplumes, their vibrant plumage a striking contrast against the softening sky.

In a remarkable display of communal spirit, the adult Gulltides bring forth their remaining food caches, a treasure trove of sustenance gathered from the rich coastal waters. With purposeful flaps of their wings, they transport an array of delicacies—seaweed and small aquatic Animara of all kinds—breaking open their bounty at the foot of the Waveplume nest in a grand gesture of solidarity and celebration.

This "leaving feast" marks a moment of abundance, with each adult Gulltide and the new prime pair of Waveplumes receiving approximately 1,000 calories each, a generous gift to sustain them on their upcoming journeys. Meanwhile, the eager chicks, filled with exuberance, dive into the offerings, gorging themselves on the feast laid before them. Each fledgling consumes around 500 calories, their small bodies quickly replenishing the energy needed for the crucial days ahead.

The air is alive with the sounds of feasting and communal bonding, a vibrant tapestry of life woven together in this sacred space as they prepare to embark on new adventures. In these final days of nurturing, the adult Gulltides demonstrate exceptional care toward their chicks, imparting essential lessons in flight. The air buzzes with excitement as the Gulltides engage in frequent flight demonstrations, their wings cutting gracefully through the air like brushstrokes on a canvas. Within a half-mile radius of the congregation, these mesmerizing displays become a captivating dance of agility and coordination, as adult birds guide their fledglings toward safe feeding areas, each flutter and glide a lesson in mastery. The fledglings, eager and wide-eyed, mimic their elders, practising short flights that carry them over the shimmering expanse of the coastal waters.

This nurturing environment ensures the next generation is well-prepared to soar into the vastness that awaits them. Beneath the watchful gaze of the new Beta pair, the vibrant tapestry of life unfolds.

As nightfall finally takes hold, the new congregation settles together, sleeping as one beneath the blanket of stars, and await the moment when the Beta Waveplumes are ready to depart, their hearts synchronised in anticipation.

Now, as our tagged Waveplumes sleep, we shall take one final look at the chicks' stats, and then that of their parents. All now rest preparing their bodies for the journey that lies ahead.

Animara Metrics Table			
	Chick 1	Chick 2	Chick 3
HP Score	90%	88%	92%
Total Flight Time	8 hours	8 hours	8 hours
Distance Travelled	55 miles	55 miles	55 miles
Calories Consumed	1.300 Cal	1.250 Cal	1.350 Cal
XP Score	2,650 XP	2,650 XP	2,700 XP
XP Needed For Next Level	Level 1 Cap (frozen for first 3 months)	Level 1 Cap (frozen for first 3 months)	Level 1 Cap (frozen for first 3 months)

In the harsh coastal world, the Gulltide chicks have grown remarkably since their hatching. Once fragile, they now exhibit significant stamina, having flown up to 55 miles in training flights and foraging journeys with their parents. Their caloric intake has increased dramatically to over 1,300 calories, vital for their continued growth.

While still bound by the early stages of life, with their XP frozen at Level 1, they have amassed 2,700 XP, preparing for future milestones. With each passing day, these young Gulltides inch closer to independence, mastering the skies they were born to forage in. Now, as we reflect on their progress, let's take one final look at their evolved parents.

Animara Metrics (FINAL EVOLUTION)	
Name: Waveplume (Male) Scientific Name: Pelecanus Oceanus Height: 160 cm (63 inches) Weight: 6,000 grams (13.23 pounds) Wingspan: 305 cm (120 inches)	Name: Waveplume (Female) Scientific Name: Pelecanus Oceanus Height: 150 cm (59 inches) Weight: 5,500 grams (12.13 pounds) Wingspan: 290 cm (114 inches)

	Male	Female	Combined
Current HP Score	135%	150% Max HP	142.5%
Total Flight Time	120 Hours	115.5 Hours	235.5 Hours
Distance Travelled	360 Miles	352.5 Miles	712.5 Miles
Calories Consumed	5,250 Cal	5,062.5 Cal	10,312.5 Cal
XP Score	11,250 XP	19,125 XP	30,375 XP
XP Needed for Next Level	22,500 XP	12,000 XP	34,500 XP

As dawn breaks over the resting Waveplumes, a serene calm blankets their coastal perch. Both birds, revitalised from their recent trials, prepare for the next leg of their journey to the new mating grounds.

The male, with 120 hours of flight time and 360 miles behind him, stretches his wings, his body now stronger with 135% HP and XP of 11,250. Beside him, the female stirs, her own flight time nearing 116 hours, having covered 352.5 miles. Her vitality is unmatched, with her HP at 150% and XP reaching an impressive 19,125.

As they rest, their combined experience signals that they will soon lead their flock to unknown territories. Their strength, sharpened by recent struggles, positions them as natural leaders. Soon, the sun will rise higher, and with it, they will set out—ready to guide their kind through the arduous journey to the new mating grounds.

As the morning light unfurls across the landscape, it casts a golden hue over the resting flock of Gulltides, stirring them gently from their slumber. One by one, bonded pairs awaken, their feathers ruffled and eyes glistening with the promise of the day ahead. Each couple shares a moment of quiet communion, the soft calls of reassurance echoing among the rocks and tide pools. The air is thick with anticipation, for the time has come for their prime pair to take to the skies and lead the flock toward new mating grounds.

Our tagged male and female Waveplumes or Beta pair, now fully revitalised, stand poised at the edge of their rocky perch. With powerful strokes of their long wings, reminiscent of majestic Albatrosses, they leap into the air. The male takes the lead, gliding effortlessly on the coastal winds, his wings outstretched to capture the warm thermals rising from the sea. The female follows closely, her keen eyes scanning the horizon for any sign of danger. Below, the rest of the flock stirs to life, their chicks watching intently as their parents take flight.

With less grace but equal enthusiasm, the younger Waveplumes mimic their elders. They launch into the air with frantic flutters, taking off from the beach, their movements marked by bursts of energy and spirited squawks. One by one, they join the rising currents, forming a lively cacophony of feathers against the brightening sky. Together, they follow their leaders, embarking on a vital journey, united in their quest for survival and new beginnings.

Chapter Forty-Two: Return to Old Friends

As the sun sinks lower, painting the sky in deep purples and fiery golds, a quiet determination fills the air. The two leading Waveplumes—male and female, their feathers shimmering in the twilight—fly in perfect unison at the head of the flock.

Beneath them, the ocean glistens in the fading light, stretching out like a mirror toward a destination known only to the pair. The male guides them with unwavering certainty. His mate soars close beside him, her keen eyes scanning the horizon as they move together with purpose.

Behind them, the flock follows, their wings beating in rhythm with the wind. To these birds, this journey feels familiar, like any other migration—a passage across the vast ocean in search of new mating grounds. They trust their new leaders without question, unaware of the deeper truth. For they are not simply flying toward a new nesting site, they are on a path that leads far beyond instinct, far beyond the ordinary, to a place of ancient mystery and an old, cherished friend.

The male and female Waveplume know this path well. They have flown it before when they first felt the pull of the Relict Forest—a land shrouded in mist and magic, where ancient waters run clear and the air hums with the weight of forgotten time. There, among the crystalline streams and towering trees, lives the Nautilix, a guardian Animara some say, and an old friend.

The Nautilix had been more than just a figure of legend to the pair. They had met before, in the quiet solitude of the Relict Forest, where the Nautilix swam gracefully through the misty rivers, its long, sinuous body gliding with effortless beauty. Back then, the Nautilix had shared its ancient wisdom, a silent, knowing presence that had comforted the then Gulltides as they navigated the mysteries of the forest. That encounter had bonded them, and now, once again, the call of the Nautilix pulls them toward the forest, toward their old friend.

As the flight draws on and the night begins to take hold, the male Waveplume lets out a soft, melodic call—a sound meant only for his mate. They both feel the same pull, the same need to return to the Relict Forest, where the Nautilix waits. Her response is quick, a sharp, echoing call of reassurance, as she glides closer to him. Together, they adjust their course slightly, angling toward the northwest, where the misty trees of the forest beckon from beyond the horizon.

Behind them, the flock remains unaware of the true nature of their journey. To them, this is just another flight, another season's migration to new lands. They follow their leaders faithfully, believing they are on the familiar path to fresh nesting grounds. But their leaders know better. They are heading not just toward survival, but toward something deeper.

One by one, the stars pierce the darkening sky, casting faint light over the ocean. The world below reflects them, creating the illusion that the flock flies between two endless expanses of starlight. But even as the beauty of the night unfolds around them, our tagged Waveplumes focus only on the path ahead. The pull grows stronger with each passing mile. They can almost feel the familiar presence of the Nautilix now, waiting patiently in the quiet, misty waters of the forest.

It is a place few have ever seen, a sanctuary hidden from time, where its Animara protector the Nautilix has watched the world change, keeping its secrets close.

To the Waveplumes, though, it is a homecoming. They know the Nautilix will greet them not as strangers but as companions, their bond forged months ago.

As they fly, the wind grows cooler. The scent of the Relict Forest is carried on the breeze—a mix of damp earth, mist, and something older, something eternal. The male and female share a look, knowing they are drawing close. The journey ahead feels both familiar and new. The male's data tag continues its steady blink, logging every mile, every change in altitude, but there is no way for it to capture the essence of what this flight truly means.

As the first light of dawn begins to edge over the horizon, softening the sky with shades of pink and blue, the Waveplumes press forward, their wings steady. The ocean below glistens with the promise of a new day, but what lies ahead remains shrouded in mystery.

The Relict Forest, the Nautilix, the reunion with their old friend — it all awaits them just beyond the horizon. What the flock will find there is unknown. Even the leaders, guided by instinct, cannot fully predict what will unfold in the heart of the forest. As they soar into the light of dawn, one thing is certain: what will happen next, as they draw near to the Nautilix and the ancient wisdom of the Relict Forest, is anyone's guess.

END

Printed in Dunstable, United Kingdom